As Autumn watched Nathan take charge, she compared him to what he'd been when they'd first met.

Then, he'd been less sure of himself. Now he was strong, assured and capable. His eyes met hers and held for a few brief moments. As if he could read her thoughts, he started toward her, paused and turned away.

To hide her confusion, Autumn got some medication for the injured horse.

"You've done a good job on this, Autumn. Having the courage to admit you lack expertise in this situation probably saved the horse for a productive future. You've done a great job, in my opinion."

Dropping her gaze, she said, "Thanks. Your opinion is important to me."

He ignored the children nearby, who looked on with interest, and drew her into his arms.

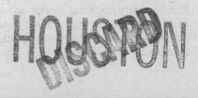

Books by Irene Brand

Love Inspired

Child of Her Heart #19
Heiress #37
To Love and Honor #49
A Groom To Come Home To #70
Tender Love #95
The Test of Love #114
Autumn's Awakening #129

IRENE BRAND

This prolific and popular author of both contemporary and historical inspirational fiction is a native of West Virginia, where she has lived all her life. She began writing professionally in 1977, after she completed her master's degree in history at Marshall University. Irene taught in secondary public schools for twenty-three years, but retired in 1989 to devote herself full-time to her writing.

In 1984, after she had enjoyed a long career of publishing articles and devotional materials, her first novel was published by Thomas Nelson. Since that time, Irene has published twenty-one contemporary and historical novels and three nonfiction titles with publishers such as Zondervan, Fleming Revell and Barbour Books.

Her extensive travels with her husband, Rod, to forty-nine of the United States and thirty-two foreign countries, have inspired much of her writing. Through her writing, Irene believes she has been helpful to others and is grateful to the many readers who have written to say that her truly inspiring stories and compelling portrayals of characters of strong faith have made a positive impression on their lives. You can write to her at P.O. Box 2770, Southside, WV 25187.

Autumn's Awakening
Irene Brand

Love Inspired®

Published by Steeple Hill Books™

STEEPLE HILL BOOKS

Steeple
Hill

ISBN 0-373-87136-8

AUTUMN'S AWAKENING

Visit us at www.steeplehill.com

Printed In U.S.A.

Therefore, if you are offering your gift at the altar and there remember that your brother has something against you, leave your gift there in front of the altar. First go and be reconciled to your brother; then come and offer your gift.

—*Matthew* 5:23-24

With special thanks to
Bill Crank, DVM (a former "A" student in my
United States history class), and his staff at the
Animal Hospital, West Virginia, for their help

and

Jim and Jackie Kessinger,
owners of Green Valley Farm, Ohio,
and their Belgian draft horses
that provided the inspiration for this book

Prologue

When daylight filtered through the open window, Autumn Weaver slipped out of bed, dressed hurriedly and walked quietly down the stairs of her family's Victorian farm home. She laid a restraining hand on the head of Spots, her border collie, when he rushed to greet her as she stepped out on the back porch. The white barn, housing her father's prize-winning Belgian horses, was barely visible through the layer of dense fog hovering over Indian Creek Farm in central Ohio.

Autumn hurried into the barn, stroking the long faces of the huge draft horses as she made her way slowly to the tack room. She heard Nathan walking around in his upstairs apartment, and she waited breathlessly until his footsteps came nearer. Nathan picked up a couple of halters before he saw her standing in the doorway.

"What are you doing here?" he demanded.

"I wanted to see you."

He brushed by her into the main passageway of the

large barn. She stopped him by placing a hand on his arm.

"After your date with Dr. Lowe last night, I didn't think you'd want to see me again," Nathan said harshly.

"I didn't have a date with him. Mother invited him to dinner. I didn't even know he was coming."

He turned to face her. "It doesn't matter anyway, Autumn. You know there can't ever be anything between us. If I can work here until the end of the month, I'll have enough money to enroll for the fall semester at the university. I'll leave then, and until that time, we'll have to stay away from each other."

"I thought you liked me, Nathan?"

He avoided her beseeching eyes. "That has nothing to do with it. Your father has made it plain that his daughters are off-limits to his hired hands. I don't blame him. In his place, I'd feel the same way."

"But we've had so much fun this summer."

"Fun we had to steal when your parents were gone. It just won't work, Autumn. Go ahead and date Dr. Lowe. He'd make a good husband for you."

"How can I date him when it's you I want?"

Her quivering lips, and the blue eyes filling with tears melted Nathan's defenses, and his determination to avoid her disappeared as though it had never been. Even as he prayed for the strength to leave her, Nathan drew Autumn close and covered her shapely mouth with his. Autumn put her arms around his neck and snuggled into his embrace. When he released her lips, she dropped her head to his shoulder with a sigh of contentment.

"I shouldn't have done that, Autumn, but I'm only human. I couldn't resist you any longer."

"Then you love me?" Autumn asked. Before he could answer, she felt a strong hand jerking backward on her shoulder. She looked up into the angry face of her father, Landon Weaver, who swung his fist and hit Nathan on the jaw.

Nathan grabbed a barn pillar to break his fall.

"Pack your things and get off this property," Landon shouted. "I'll figure out what I owe you and send it to your uncle's farm. Don't ever let me see your face around here again. I told you to stay away from my daughter."

"Tell her to stay away from *me*. I didn't ask her to come here this morning," Nathan protested. "This hasn't happened before."

"That's a likely story," Landon said. "My daughters don't pursue farmhands."

Nathan faced Autumn, and she was touched by the distress in his voice.

"Tell him! Tell him I've never kissed you before."

Autumn looked from Nathan's bruised face and troubled gray eyes to the father she loved more than any other person in the world. As long as she could remember, she'd tagged her father's heels until she knew as much about the Belgian horses and the farm operation as Landon himself knew. Always before, Landon had given her everything she wanted, but from the belligerent gleam in his eyes, she knew he wouldn't let her have Nathan.

She looked again at Nathan, whom she adored with all the fervor of an eighteen-year-old's first love. She'd only known Nathan Holland a few months. Could she choose him over her father? Without considering the far-reaching consequence of her action, Autumn took one last look at Nathan and walked out of the barn without saying a word in his defense.

Chapter One

Blinded by the sudden onslaught of water across the windshield, Autumn braked sharply when an eighteen-wheeler passed her. She flipped the wipers to the highest speed and straightened in the car seat. Numb from hunching over the steering wheel for hours, she considered asking Trina to drive, but it was too risky to stop and change drivers on the interstate. Besides, Trina was asleep, and she was wide awake. Thoughts of the past had kept her wakeful since they'd passed Indianapolis.

When Autumn Weaver left Ohio eight years ago, she hadn't intended to return to Greensboro. She couldn't imagine why she'd allowed Ray Wheeler to talk her into taking over his veterinary practice for two months. Was it possible that she hoped for reconciliation with her family? To ask forgiveness for her misguided decisions? To atone for the way she'd disillusioned and disappointed her parents and had caused Nathan Holland to lose his job at Indian Creek Farm?

More than once since she and her closest friend,

Trina, had left Wisconsin, Autumn had been tempted to telephone Ray and tell him she'd changed her mind. The bitter incidents that had caused her to leave home had dominated her thoughts for years, but Autumn realized that sometime she would have to deal with the past. Perhaps that time had come.

When she caught herself nodding off, Autumn reached a hand and touched Trina lightly on the shoulder. Trina was a sound sleeper, and when she didn't stir, Autumn shook her gently.

Trina stretched. "Are we there yet?"

"Not for another two or three hours. I should have telephoned Ray that we'd be late, but by that time, he would already have left for the airport."

"What time is it?" Trina asked, riffling in her purse for her glasses.

"Midnight."

"Maybe we ought to stop for the night. There should be a motel at the next exit."

"Do you have enough money for a motel bill?" Autumn asked.

Yawning widely, Trina said, "I've got a hundred dollars."

"I have about half that much, and I don't want to spend it on a motel when there's a free bed waiting for us in Greensboro. We'd better go on."

"Do you want me to drive?"

"I'll be all right if you'll stay awake and talk to me. Otherwise, I might fall asleep and run off the road."

Trina ran a pick through her short brown hair and took a swig from a water bottle. She handed Autumn a granola bar. "Eat this, and it'll perk you up." She glanced at her six-year-old niece curled up on the back seat of Autumn's old car. "Dolly is sound asleep."

Trina inserted a tape in the player and the music of her favorite gospel singer filled the car. Through the words of the songwriter, the singer asked God to forgive her if she had wounded anyone with her wilful ways.

As Trina hummed the lyrics, Autumn considered her friend's strong Christian faith that had kept both of them optimistic during years of difficulties. Trina's daily prayers on her behalf had brought a semblance of peace to Autumn's life, and calmness out of the chaos the two friends shared as they worked their way through the veterinary school at the University of Wisconsin.

"Sorry I went to sleep and left you alone with your thoughts," Trina said. "Have they been pleasant?"

"Not particularly. I've been thinking about the summer I left Ohio, wondering why I was foolish enough to return."

"I believe it's the providence of God. It wasn't a coincidence that we met Doc Wheeler at that veterinarians' convention. Whether you were right or wrong, you can't have peace of mind and experience the full love of God in your heart until you come to terms with the past. Our temporary jobs as Wheeler's assistants will give you time to make up with your family and set things right with Nathan Holland."

"I don't even know where Nathan went to when he left Greensboro."

"Did you ask Doc Wheeler about Nathan?"

"No. Doc surprised me so much when he told me he was taking a world tour, I didn't ask any questions. To my knowledge, he's never traveled overseas. Before I recovered from my surprise, I agreed to take over for him. He has a large practice, so I'm glad he wanted you to come along, too.''

Conversation ceased and the tires hummed as they hit the concrete in steady rhythm. The lyrics of the song once more infiltrated Autumn's thoughts: ''If I have wounded any soul today.'' *It's not "if", God. You know how many people I've wounded.*

''The things Ray told me about my family are worrying me. I can't believe they've changed so much since I left home.''

''You've been gone eight years! A lot of things can happen in that time.''

''But I can't imagine Mother as an invalid, confined to a wheelchair. And it's hard to believe that the six years she's been sick, Daddy has lost interest in the farm. If Ray is right about how run-down the farm is, and I'm sure he wouldn't have told me if he hadn't known, it'll hurt me to see it.''

''Didn't he say your sister is living at home? Maybe she's taken over.''

''Not Summer! She's a quiet, shy person, who prefers indoor activities. I was the tomboy who followed Daddy around the farm.''

Punching a button to clear steam from the windshield, Autumn looked at the highway markers. ''We leave the interstate at the next exit, then it's a short drive to Greensboro.'' She handed Trina the granola wrapper to put in the trash bag. ''That did liven me up. Let's stop at a restaurant for a cup of coffee, and I'll be okay until we get to our destination.''

''Not a very lively town,'' Trina observed as they drove along Greensboro's main street an hour later.

The rain had lessened somewhat, but dense fog obscured the streetlights and the business section resembled an eerie scene in a Hallowe'en movie.

"It never has been," Autumn agreed, but she looked fondly at the stores and office buildings. They passed the high school where she'd graduated, and she remembered the years she'd been the star of the girls' basketball team. Her sisters, Spring and Summer, had been cheerleaders, but because of her height, she'd considered herself too gauche to try out as a cheerleader.

"Things haven't changed much, except for the new shopping mall we passed on the outskirts of town. Apparently, it hasn't hurt the downtown merchants, for most of these businesses are still operating."

"Where's your home?" Trina asked. "Did we pass it?"

"No. Indian Creek Farm is south of Greensboro about ten miles." They crossed a bridge, and the headlights illuminated a muddy creek, running bank full. "Apparently, it's been a wet spring. The grass looks lush and green. Every year while I've been away, I've thought of how the farm would be changing with the seasons. I liked spring best of all."

Yes, she liked spring, although she had to admit that winter was also a favorite time because she'd first met Nathan in the midst of a snowstorm. Every mile she'd come closer to Greensboro rapidly brought memories of Nathan to the foreground of her mind. Things about him she hadn't remembered for years had surfaced. Coming home may have been the greatest mistake of her life.

Autumn turned into a driveway beside a two-story frame house with a low, long building attached to the rear of the residence. "Here we are," she said. "That's the animal clinic in back."

"The house is dark," Trina said. "Maybe we aren't expected."

"Ray and his sister, Olive, live together, but she's probably gone to bed." Flashing her car lights on bright, Autumn said, "There's a note on the door. It's probably for us. Wait in the car until I find out."

Pulling on her raincoat, Autumn got out of the car and ran up the steps. The note was addressed to her, so she pulled it off the screen and hurried back to the car.

"Dear Autumn," Olive had written. "It's midnight, and I'm going to bed. The door is unlocked, and your two rooms are upstairs on the right side of the hall. You and your friend will share the bath between your rooms. Make yourself at home. Wake me if you need help. Olive."

Using a flashlight, taking only two small bags, and supporting the drowsy Dolly between them, Autumn and Trina moved into the central hallway of the house.

"Should we lock the door behind us?" Trina whispered.

"Not many people in Greensboro lock their doors, so don't bother." Tiptoeing quietly up the wooden stair treads wasn't easy, but they didn't awaken Olive. "You and Dolly take the rear bedroom," Autumn said.

"Okay. Wake me in the morning when you want to get up."

"It's almost two o'clock now, so let's sleep late if we can."

For weeks Autumn had been dreading the return to her childhood haunts, and now that she was finally here, she doubted she would sleep, but an antique wooden bed with white sheets, covered with one of Olive Wheeler's handmade quilts, looked inviting. Autumn pulled off her denim shorts and cotton shirt, slipped into a cotton nightshirt and snuggled beneath the fresh scented covers.

God, she prayed, *I feel sort of like Jacob in the Old Testament, who'd run away to escape the wrath of his brother. Jacob returned a rich man, and I've come home penniless. So maybe I'm more like the prodigal son, who came back home wanting his father's forgiveness. Will Daddy be as willing to forgive as the father in the parable? Will I have the nerve to approach him and ask forgiveness? Maybe I won't be able to make up with my family, but I want to. You know there's never been a day I haven't missed them. Even if I can't be received back into the good graces of my parents, it still feels good to be home.*

In spite of her unpleasant memories, incessant rain dripping on the tin roof soon lulled Autumn into a sense of peace, forgetfulness and sleep.

"Autumn! Autumn!" A quiet voice intruded into her thoughts, and she sat up in bed, momentarily forgetting where she was. A soft knock sounded at the door.

"Come in!" she said, and Olive Wheeler opened the door. Autumn blinked when she turned on the ceiling light.

"When did you get in, Autumn?" she asked. "I didn't hear you."

"About half-past two. What time is it now?"

"Four o'clock. I hate to bother you, but I've had a

call from one of Ray's good customers, so I think you or your friend ought to check it out.''

Swinging out of bed, Autumn said, ''I'll go. Trina doesn't know anything about this country, and she'd never find her way tonight. Besides, we brought her niece with us, and Trina should be here if Dolly awakens in a strange house.'' Pulling a pair of jeans and a long-sleeved shirt out of her bag, she asked, ''What's wrong, and where am I going?'' Olive answered the second question first, and her words, ''Woodbeck Farm,'' halted Autumn with one long leg in her jeans, the other still bare. Matthew Holland, Nathan's uncle, owned Woodbeck Farm! Why was the first call as Ray's assistant to a place that dug up best-forgotten memories?

She finished dressing and followed Olive downstairs to the clinic. ''What's wrong?''

''The boy who called said the cow had fallen down in the pasture field, and Mr. Holland thinks she has grass tetany. This happens to cows lots of times in a wet season.'' She unlocked a large refrigerator. ''Ray keeps all his drugs in there. Do you know what to take?''

''Yes. A lot of my clinical work was among dairy herds in Wisconsin. You go back to bed, Miss Olive, I'll manage all right.''

Olive opened a desk drawer and handed Autumn a set of keys. ''The truck's in the garage.'' Before she left the room, the angular woman peered up at Autumn, eyes compassionate, above a long, bony nose. ''I think Ray put you on the spot to ask you to come back here, Autumn, but now that you have, I hope everything works out for the best. They may not admit it, but your family needs you." She gave Autumn a quick hug before she went back to bed.

Autumn had often helped Ray Wheeler with his veterinary work, and she'd been in and out of the Wheeler house often. Apparently Olive and Ray had remained Autumn's friends when her family and other neighbors had been quick to judge her, for Ray had been friendly when she'd seen him last month. Now Olive's compassion brought a lump to Autumn's throat. But she'd become adept at stifling her heartaches, so she gathered up several bottles of drugs and dropped them in a plastic bucket. Ray's work clothes hung in the garage, and Autumn stepped into a pair of none-too-clean coveralls, took off her sneakers and pulled on a pair of Ray's rubber boots. She found a wide-brimmed rain hat to put on when she got to the farm.

This wouldn't have been an easy assignment under any circumstances, but she wasn't sure she was ready to meet Nathan's uncle. She'd hoped, while she was in Greensboro, to learn what Nathan had been doing since she'd seen him, but was she ready to learn that he was married and had a family? The thought had ruined her peace of mind for years. That knowledge would hurt, but on the other hand, if, as Trina insisted, Autumn needed something to put a lid on the past, Nathan, happily married, should do it.

Autumn drove carefully to avoid ponding water on the narrow secondary road. After she'd driven for eight miles, a large sign at the roadside pointed the way: Woodbeck Farm, half mile. When she reached the farm buildings, a boy emerged from the shelter of a shed. Stifling a yawn, he stood by the car door when she got out.

"I'm Tony Simpson. Mr. Holland's out in the field with the sick cow. He told me to fetch you."

Autumn took the bucket of supplies out of the car, and carrying a flashlight, she followed Tony into the darkness.

She heard Indian Creek tumbling along its course, but so far, the stream hadn't overflowed its banks. The soil beneath the grass was soft and spongy, and when they reached a muddy, grassless area, Autumn's feet flew out from under her. She sat down suddenly in the muck. Tony didn't even know she'd fallen and he plodded onward.

After a quick examination, Autumn decided that nothing was broken, so she struggled to her feet in the slick mud and hurried to keep the boy in sight. All in the life of a vet, she figured, remembering the times they'd called for Doc Wheeler to come to Indian Creek Farm in the middle of the night.

A lantern burned in the distance, and Tony shouted, "The doc's here."

Covered with a hooded raincoat, a man knelt in the mud beside a cow. The large animal's wet black coat glistened in the dim light as it bellowed and struggled with severe paddling convulsions.

"I believe your diagnosis of grass tetany is right, Mr. Holland," Autumn said, observing the symptoms of a disease found in cows that fed on luxuriant, rapidly growing pasture in the spring, leading to a chemical imbalance. She pulled a stethoscope from the bucket and knelt beside the large animal. "I'll listen to her heart."

The farmer quickly lifted his head and peered at her from under the hood. The lantern's light shone on his face. For a few breathtaking moments, Autumn was speechless, then she whispered, ''Nathan?''

''Autumn!''

She pushed back the brim of her hat, and the rain streamed over her face. The cow forgotten for the moment, each stared at the other. Autumn's heartbeat swelled with wonder, thankfulness and affection as she laid her hand tenderly on the shoulder of this man she couldn't forget. A man she never expected to see again.

''So you became a vet after all?''

She grinned slightly. ''Just last week. And I've got a little piece of paper to prove it.''

He reached out his hand and she placed hers in it.

''Welcome home, Autumn,'' Nathan said, and Autumn felt that she *really* had come home.

Chapter Two

One of the cow's flailing hooves struck Autumn's leg, and remembering why she was here, she put her stethoscope on the animal's trembling side. The loud palpitations hurt her ears. She handed the stethoscope to Nathan so he could hear the hammering heart, wondering if he could also detect her pulse beating almost as fast as the cow's.

"I'm sure it's grass tetany," she explained, "but Ray has plenty of medicines, so I hope it's not too late to save her."

"I didn't find her until after dark," Nathan said, concern in his voice. "She was bawling and galloping around blindly before she fell down. I haven't had this happen to any of my cattle before. What can you do?"

"I'll slowly inject her with a mixture of magnesium and calcium compounds and monitor the heart carefully while I'm doing it. If she reacts favorably, I'll administer a sedative to settle her down so we can take her into shelter. All of this rain has increased the po-

tassium and nitrogen in the herbage, so she needs to
be taken out of the pasture.''

After an hour or so, the cow seemed stable, so Autumn, Nathan, and Tony urged her to her feet and
alternately led and pushed her toward the barn. After
the animal was bedded down in a sawdust-littered
stall, Autumn said, ''You should feed her hay and concentrate for the next few days to keep the blood magnesium from falling again. I'll come back later on today and bring some more medication for you to give
her every day.''

Exhausted, the boy curled up on a stack of hay and
went to sleep. Nathan grinned. ''Tony's not used to
working all night. He's a neighbor boy, who helps me
occasionally. His parents are gone and he was spending the night with me, but he hasn't gotten much
sleep.'' Nathan shook the boy's shoulder. ''Tony,
come in the house and go to bed.'' Tony didn't stir.
Nathan took a blanket off a hook and covered the boy
with it. ''The night's almost over, so I might as well
let him sleep here.''

The rain had ceased and daylight had come when
they left the barn. ''So you're the assistant Ray hired
while he took a two-months' world tour. Wonder why
he didn't tell me you were the one?''

''I thought you were surprised to see me. Didn't
Ray tell anyone that I was helping him for a few
weeks?''

''If he had, I'm sure I would have heard that the
runaway Weaver daughter was coming home.''

Autumn was tired, and she didn't like the cynical
tone of his voice, wondering if Nathan had changed
for the worse since she'd seen him. He'd been a shy,
soft-spoken, understanding youth. She opened the door

of Ray's truck, pulled off the muddy coveralls and put them and the bucket of supplies on the floor of the cab.

"Do you want to come in for breakfast and a cup of coffee?" he said in a matter-of-fact voice.

Autumn hesitated. She'd only be in Greensboro for two months, so was it wise to open up old wounds? But she couldn't turn down an opportunity to find out about Nathan. Was he married? Was he inviting her to eat on behalf of his wife? There was one way to find out, so she said, "Yes. I'd like that."

She followed him up two steps to the back porch, and when he held the door open, she entered the kitchen, a large, squarish room, with an oval wooden table in the center. One corner of the room held a television, a plastic-covered lounge chair and a matching sofa. The room smacked of masculinity. Although it was neat and orderly, Autumn didn't see any evidence that a woman lived there—no floral arrangements, no feminine apparel, no knickknacks on the shelves. At the sink, Nathan ran water into a teakettle and took cooking utensils from a cabinet, as if he knew his way around the kitchen. No wife now, Autumn was sure, but had there been one in the years since she'd known him?

Until the warmth of the room reached out to comfort her, Autumn hadn't realized she was shaking from the dampness. Or was it a reaction to his unexpected presence? Nathan directed her to the washroom near the kitchen, and when she returned, he had two plates laid, and eggs and bacon frying.

"Where's your uncle?" she asked.

"He died two years ago and willed the farm to me. I've been living here for a year and a half."

Her eyes widened in surprise. When she was a girl, she'd admitted to Doc Wheeler that she had a serious crush on Nathan. Why hadn't he mentioned that Nathan was now the owner of Woodbeck Farm?

Autumn watched Nathan as he worked. Above his straight, wide eyebrows, the years had marked his face with a network of deeply etched lines. His forehead ran freely into the structure of a high-bridged nose. He still wore his dark-brown hair short and his slate-gray eyes were calm but guarded when he looked at her. Nathan had been unsure of himself and exhibited a low self-esteem when he'd first come to work at Indian Creek Farm, but while they had worked with the sick cow tonight, she'd been impressed by his confidence and skill.

If memories of the slender, youthful Nathan had kept her from being interested in any other man, what effect would a brawny, mature Nathan have on her? Nathan's shirt stretched tightly over well-muscled arms and shoulders, and his hands were quick and deft at his tasks.

God, is Trina right? Could Nathan be the reason You brought me back to Greensboro?

Nathan placed two eggs, bacon and three slices of toast on her plate. "Do you take your coffee black?"

"Yes, and the stronger the better. I started drinking coffee in vet school. After I worked and studied most of the night, I needed something to keep me awake."

He looked keenly at her. In some ways she looked as he'd remembered her. Curly auburn shoulder-length hair always falling carelessly over her brow. Keen, azure eyes on a level with his. Above-medium height that matched his own. These physical characteristics hadn't changed. What was missing?

Enthusiasm that had marked her youth had been replaced by resignation. Once he could detect what Autumn was thinking by looking at her, but her steady gaze was unfathomable now. There was a new maturity about her. Dark circles under her eyes indicated a strain that was more than skin deep and her smooth pinkish complexion was marred by slight worry creases across her forehead. When she relaxed, she looked tired.

Autumn squirmed under his intense scrutiny and he said, "You're too thin. Have you had a rough time?"

"I guess you could say that. Working my way through three years of college and four years of vet school wasn't easy."

The food was tasty, and they ceased conversation until their appetites were sated. Nathan replenished their coffee cups and leaned back in his chair.

"I didn't know you'd left Greensboro until I came back after my uncle's death."

Autumn looked out the window where early-morning sunlight revealed a verdant meadow. A herd of about thirty Angus cattle grazed contentedly. A meadowlark softly greeted the morning from a fence post. She wondered if it was too soon to stir up the past, to speak of incidents best forgotten.

"I left Ohio the day after you did, and I haven't been back since. I'm not sure I should have come home now."

"Why? Because I'm here?"

"That has nothing to do with it," she declared, thinking if she'd known he was at Woodbeck Farm, she might have returned sooner. "What did you do before you inherited the farm?"

"After the things that happened between—" he

paused ''—between us, I wanted to put as much space between me and Ohio as possible. I got a job in the Middle East oil fields. I'd probably still be there if Uncle Matt hadn't died and willed me this property.''

He paused momentarily, remembering the lonely years he'd worked hard, long hours trying to force his fascination for Autumn from his heart. He'd thought he'd succeeded, but now that he'd seen her again, he knew his efforts had been wasted. The affection he'd thought was gone had only been buried, for it had surfaced the minute he'd seen her tonight.

''But I made a lot of money,'' he continued. ''I sent some to help my mother and banked the rest, so I had some capital to get started. Uncle Matt hadn't been in good health for a few years, and the place was really run-down. It will take a long time, and lots of work and money, to get the farm the way I want it to be.''

Autumn remembered his dream of becoming a farmer, and she was happy that he'd reached his goal. She toyed with the coffee cup, refusing when he wanted to refill it.

''I'd better go. There's probably lots of calls to make, and I don't want to put the whole burden on Trina.''

''Who?''

''Trina Jackson. She's my friend, and we went through school together. She'll be helping out until Ray gets back.'' She thanked him for breakfast and stood up.

''Sit down, Autumn. You can spare a few more minutes. I've told you what I've been doing. I'm curious about you.''

Reluctant to talk about the past, but even more reluctant to leave him, she settled back into the chair.

Without meeting his eyes, she said, "When I confessed to Daddy that I—" she hesitated, and chose different words "—was interested in you, he was so angry, he threatened to cut off all my funds until I came to my senses. My mother wanted me to marry Harrison Lowe. She was ambitious for her daughters, and when Harrison showed some interest in me, she decided I'd make a good doctor's wife."

"But you wanted to be a veterinarian."

"That's true. I'd wanted to be a vet since I was a child and had seen Doc Wheeler save one of our colts. I wasn't surprised that Mother would disagree, but I was sure Daddy would be on my side. He always had been before."

Autumn paused, recalling the year she'd been spent in an expensive boarding school in the East. Her parents' plans to prepare her for a social life had ebbed when she came home for the Christmas holidays and met Nathan. By the end of the first year, she'd made up her mind that she wouldn't return to the boarding school—a decision that had intensified when she reached the farm and found Nathan working for her father.

Wondering what Autumn was thinking that had caused sadness to overspread her face, Nathan recalled that his uncle had told him how disappointed the Weavers had been when their oldest daughter, Spring, had married a missionary and moved to Bolivia. The second daughter, Summer, was a shy girl, and Clara Weaver was determined that Autumn would be trained to carry on the aristocratic Weaver tradition. Had his appearance in her life caused Autumn to rebel against her parents? Nathan wondered how much he was responsible for changing the vivacious, laughing girl he'd known into this serious woman with a resigned look on her face.

"Harrison was all right, but I didn't want to marry him, and I wasn't going to fight with Mother about it. When I learned you'd gone without even saying good-bye, I left, too. I didn't tell anyone where I was going. As a matter of fact, I didn't know what I was going to do when I drove away from Greensboro."

She paused, and the bleak expression in her eyes deepened as she remembered vividly the lost, hopeless feeling she'd experienced that day.

"So what did you do?"

She laughed slightly and the sparkle in her blue eyes dissolved some of the fatigue lines on her face. "I decided to travel. Trina is a cousin of Bert Brown, who's married to my sister, Spring. Trina and I met at their wedding, and we kept in touch by letter after that. She'd invited me to visit her, and when I had no other place to go, I went to see her in Nashville. I took all the money from my savings account that I'd been accumulating since I was a child, and when I got to Columbus I sold my sports car. I had enough money to last me for a while."

"I remember that sports car! Wasn't it hard to give up?"

"Not really. Daddy bought it for me when I graduated from high school. I wanted a pickup truck instead, but Mother objected that it wasn't a suitable vehicle for me, so they gave me an expensive car. When I needed money, I was glad I had it. Trina was getting ready to go to a Christian youth conference in London, and since I had nothing else to do, I tagged along."

Autumn paused, thinking about the conference that

had introduced her to a whole new way of life. Trina had jokingly called her a heathen, because she knew nothing about what it meant to be a Christian. Except for a few weddings and funerals, Autumn had never attended a church service, but after she spent two weeks at that conference, she'd become a student of the Bible, trying to span her gulf of ignorance about spiritual matters. She'd come to believe the Gospel message, but even yet, she couldn't submit wholly to Christ's lordship. Looking at Nathan's interested eyes across the table, she knew she couldn't expect God to forgive her own sins until she'd received forgiveness from Nathan and her parents for the past.

"And then what?" Nathan prompted.

"After the conference, with a group of youths and a couple of adult advisors, we backpacked several months on the continent of Europe. We'd travel until we ran out of money, then we'd find work, usually on farms. Trina was a city girl, but she became interested in animals, and we decided to go to vet school. I had $5.25 in my pocket when I got off the plane in Milwaukee."

"How did you manage to go to college? Did your father help you?"

"I've had no contact with my family since I left. I learned through my sister, Spring, that Daddy had disowned me, saying I would never be welcome at Indian Creek Farm again. I guess I'm as stubborn as he is, so I didn't ask him for anything."

"You didn't know your mother is ill?"

"Not until I saw Ray last month. He told me she's an invalid and also how Daddy has let the farm run down. Those are the reasons I said I might have been better off to stay away. I can't bear to think of my home and family deteriorating when there's nothing I can do about it.''

"Where did you go to school?'' Nathan asked, wanting to learn everything he could about those years Autumn had been lost to him.

"At the University of Wisconsin.''

"Why Wisconsin?''

"Trina's sister lives in Milwaukee, and after we got back from Europe, she offered us a place to stay until we got settled. Too, it was far enough away from Ohio that I didn't think I'd encounter anyone I knew.''

"That school has a good reputation.''

Autumn nodded. "I already had one year of college, and some of my credits were accepted at Wisconsin. By taking classes year-round, we graduated last month. There were times when I wondered if I'd ever graduate, for, to pay our expenses, Trina and I started a cleaning business. We hired other students to work for us. We cleaned office buildings at night, and we didn't have much time to study.''

"And your father sitting here with his pockets full of money!''

"If I'd done what my parents wanted, they'd have taken care of me, but I didn't choose to do that.'' She stood up and stretched. "Thanks for the breakfast. I'll check on the cow, and then I'll head back to Greensboro.''

He walked with her to the barn, where they found Tony still sleeping on the hay, and the cow contentedly chewing her cud.

"You saved the cow for me, Autumn, and I appreciate your coming to help. I can't afford to lose any livestock. I'm operating on a shoestring.'' He took her hand in a firm shake. "You're going to be a good vet.

I'm glad you had the courage to get what you wanted in life.''

Not everything I wanted, she thought, for she'd never gotten over losing him. She wouldn't meet Nathan's gaze, fearing he could read the emotion in her eyes.

As they strolled toward the truck, Nathan said, ''Hearing your story has cleared up something that's bothered me since I came to Greensboro. It took me months to convince people that you and I hadn't been living together the years I was away.''

Autumn stared at him. ''What?''

''That's right. And I understand why now. If you left the day after I did, and no one knew where either of us was, they jumped to a wrong conclusion. I wouldn't have mentioned it, but someone might say something to you.''

''I won't be here very long, so perhaps I won't have to answer questions about my past.''

Nathan watched as she got into Ray's truck and started the engine. Before she drove away, Autumn looked directly into his gray eyes and said, ''I don't expect you to forgive me, Nathan, but that day after Daddy fired you, I told him that I was to blame for what happened between us. He didn't believe me, but as soon as I could, I came to Woodbeck Farm. By that time you were already gone, and your uncle wouldn't tell me where you were. There was no way to make restitution, but I've always wanted to see you again and tell you I was sorry.''

He held up his hand. ''Don't be so hard on yourself, Autumn. I was as much to blame as you. We were both too young to be making decisions for the future. It's okay.''

"I hope so. Anyway, I'm thankful that God brought us together again so I could apologize."

He nodded, and the warmth in his steady, gray eyes made her hopeful. "It's good to see you again. Autumn."

Chapter Three

When Autumn reached the highway, she took the long way back to Greensboro. She had to deal with this surprise meeting with Nathan before she talked to Trina or Miss Olive. In spite of the lack of sleep she'd had, Autumn couldn't remember when she'd felt so exhilarated. After being empty for eight years, a part of her had suddenly been filled when Nathan took her hand and said, "Welcome home, Autumn."

What had drawn her to Nathan in the first place? What had captivated her so forcefully that no other man had ever seemed worthy of her attention? With the window down, and the wind fluffing her curly red hair around her face, she drove slowly over roads that had been familiar to her in the past.

Perhaps one reason she cherished his friendship was that he'd come into her life on a Christmas Eve when she desperately needed help. Her father was returning from a Belgian horse association meeting. Her mother, Clara, and sister, Summer, had gone to the airport to meet him, while Autumn stayed at home. A freak snowstorm had delayed Landon's flight, and Clara and Summer were marooned at the airport.

Resigned to spending Christmas Eve alone, Autumn had turned on the in-house monitoring system that Landon used to survey what was going on in the horse barns. Autumn loved watching the horses. She scanned the huge, well-lit barn with its comfortable box stalls, the huge reddish horses munching slowly on their supper of oats mixed with molasses. All seemed well until she looked at Tulip in the last stall. Instead of eating, Landon's prize brood mare paced restlessly, acting colicky. Landon Weaver's horses didn't get the colic, and Autumn had known immediately what was wrong. Tulip was getting ready to foal.

Autumn had telephoned for the veterinarian immediately, only to learn from Miss Olive that Ray Wheeler was out on a call. Under ordinary conditions, the mare could deliver her foal without any assistance, but if there was trouble, it could mean the loss of the mare or foal. Autumn drew on heavy clothes and fought her way to the barn through the swirling snow. She'd helped her father many times when a mare needed assistance, but she was afraid to try it by herself.

Autumn was busily preparing the foaling stall, when a slender young man walked into the barn. Pulling a red snow-covered cap from his dark-brown hair, he'd said in a hesitant voice, "I'm Nathan Holland. I'm visiting my uncle at Woodbeck Farm, and he volunteered my assistance to clean the barns while Mr. Weaver's been gone. Uncle was afraid this storm would delay your father's return, and he asked me to drive over and check on the horses."

"Oh, I'm so glad to see you," Autumn said, warming to the sincerity in his slate-gray eyes and the slight smile on his sensitive, well-formed mouth. "One of the horses is going to foal, and I need help."

He laughed lowly, and Autumn liked the sound. "Shouldn't you call a vet? I'm a city boy. I won't be much help."

"I can tell you what to do," Autumn had assured him, and the two of them had worked companionably as they padded the foaling stall and moved the large Belgian into place. Then they'd gone into Landon's office to monitor the mare's progress on the television screen. While they munched on snacks Autumn had found in the refrigerator, she had told Nathan of her desire to be a vet.

"Seems like that would be a good job for you," he'd said. "I'd go for it."

"What would you like to do, Nathan?" she'd asked, for they'd started out on a first-name basis.

"Since I graduated from high school, I've been working at a plant in Indianapolis," he said, "helping to support my mother and brothers, and I haven't thought much about the future." He laughed, embarrassed, as he added, "But working here for your father the past few days, I've decided I'd like to be a farmer."

"I can't think of any better profession," Autumn told him. "I'd love to spend the rest of my life here on the farm."

"But to be a successful farmer, I'd need to go to college, and I don't have any money for that nor to buy a farm. It's only a dream."

"It doesn't have to be," she'd said. "My great-grandfather started the Weaver Belgian tradition with one filly. He didn't have any money to buy stock, but a man gave him an orphan foal the owner thought was going to die. He nursed the filly until it was well, and the rest of the story is all around us. I've been taught to believe you can have anything you *really* want.''

Their conversation was interrupted when she'd discovered that Tulip was having trouble. Autumn had spent the next hour moving the foal into position for birth. Nathan had knelt beside her, helping and encouraging her in every way he could. Soon after midnight, Tulip had given birth to a healthy filly, a sleek auburn-brown foal with a pronounced star in the long white streak down its nose. Landon had been so grateful that Autumn had saved both the mare and foal that he'd given the foal to her as a Christmas gift. She'd promptly named the filly Noel to commemorate the day of its birth.

The next day Nathan had gone home to Indianapolis, and at the end of the holidays, Autumn went back to college. She didn't forget Nathan, however, and during the winter, she'd made two decisions that had plunged her into conflict with her parents and had charted her future course. She would not return to the fancy boarding school, and she intended to find out where Nathan was so she could pursue their acquaintance.

Elated over her chance meeting with Nathan at Woodbeck Farm, Autumn entered the Wheeler home through the kitchen. Dolly and Trina sat at a round table, that had served several generations of Wheelers, feasting on pancakes and sausage. Autumn had hesitated about bringing Dolly, fearing Olive wouldn't want an uninvited guest, but Ray's sister had already succumbed to Dolly's chatter and winning smile. Dolly was a chubby child, and her long brown hair framed a dark oval face dominated by slate-gray eyes. Dolly was cheerful and lovable.

"Come and have pancakes, Autumn," Dolly called. "Miss Olive is a good cook."

"I enjoyed Miss Olive's meals before you were born," Autumn said, ruffling Dolly's hair. "I need a shower before anything else. Besides, I've already had my breakfast."

"You're looking decidedly cheerful for a woman who drove five hundred miles yesterday and spent most of the night out on a vet call," Trina observed.

Olive laughed, Autumn blushed and Trina stared suspiciously at her friend.

Heading for the stairs, Autumn said, "I'll be down soon. Do we have a full schedule today?"

"Only a few calls so far. Ray's usual procedure is to open the clinic for surgery at eight o'clock," Olive explained, "and go on field calls in the afternoon. Since there are two of you, it should work out well for one of you to be at the clinic all the time. We have lots of emergency walk-in customers. Ray is the only vet in the area, so he's always busy."

"Suits us," Trina said. "We need to put our education to practical use."

When Autumn got back to her room after showering, Trina was struggling up the stairs with two suitcases.

"I'll help with that," Autumn said, "as soon as I dress."

"Take your time. Dolly is helping Miss Olive with the dishes." Trina brought a bag into Autumn's room. She admired an antique barrel-top train trunk that stood in front of the window, then sat on the side of Autumn's bed.

"You look happier than I've seen you since the day Spring and Bert were married. What's happened?"

Pulling a sweatshirt over her head, Autumn grinned. "Old eagle eye! Am I *that* transparent?" Her pulse quickened when she said happily, "My early-morning call was to the farm of Nathan Holland. His uncle died and Nathan inherited the property that adjoins Daddy's farm."

"No wonder you're radiant! Don't tell me you've already patched up the differences of the past."

Autumn shook her head. "We're a long way from that, for we can't span eight years in a few hours. He did ask me to have breakfast with him, so I suppose that's a step in the right direction."

"Apparently that torch you've carried for him is still burning brightly?"

"I don't know how bright it is, but there's still a flicker left. It's ridiculous, with all that's behind me and the future I have as a veterinarian, that I can't forget a girlish infatuation."

"Are you sure it was only an infatuation?"

"I don't know, but I suppose two months will give me time to find out." Autumn finished tying her shoes. "Let's go to work."

Nathan jammed his hands deep in his pockets as Autumn drove away from Woodbeck Farm. He returned to the kitchen, filled the dishwasher, unlocked a drawer in his desk and took out a large envelope. Sitting at the table, he drew out a photograph that he'd mistakenly taken away from Indian Creek Farm the day Landon had fired him. As he'd angrily scooped up his possessions and loaded them into boxes, he didn't realize he'd gotten a file folder that belonged to the Weavers.

After he arrived at the oil camp in the Middle East, he started studying the textbooks and notes he'd used at OSU, where he had studied for one semester. Among his papers, he'd discovered a folder containing several newspaper clippings of Weaver triumphs at various fairs and farm shows. Triumphs that had made the Weaver girls famous throughout the Midwest. Their names commemorating the seasons of the year had been noteworthy, but from the time they were able to walk, dressed alike in prairie dresses and sunbonnets, they'd perched on the wagon beside their father as his six-hitch draft horses won numerous trophies in parades and fairs in Ohio and neighboring states.

The enclosure that ruined what little peace of mind Nathan had mustered since the episode with Landon was a large photo of Autumn, dressed in a long, blue dress, wearing a matching sunbonnet, standing beside a Belgian mare. Nathan was angry that her image had followed him halfway around the world, and he started to destroy the picture, but he didn't have the courage. Posting her picture over his bunk, he learned to live with Autumn's presence, thinking he would never see her again.

"God," he moaned, "why did she have to come back? I've ordered my life without her and am finally making something of myself. The things that matter the most haven't changed. I'm still a struggling farmer born on the wrong side of the tracks. She's Autumn Weaver, member of a socially prominent family and possible heir to great riches. Why did she have to return?"

But had he ordered his life without her? Determined to wipe Autumn's memory from his mind, Nathan had dated several women, but none of them snagged his interest. Nathan thought Autumn was the most beautiful girl he'd ever seen, and all other women paled into insignificance when he compared them to Autumn when she was eighteen. She'd been tall, willowy, regal. Curly chestnut hair framed her oval face like a halo, and her animated sky-blue eyes nestled in a smooth, creamy complexion, soft as a rose petal. She was even more fascinating now. Nathan shook his head to clear away the memories and locked the picture back in his desk.

He went to the barn and took the still-sleeping Tony by the arm. "Wake up, Tony. Your mother told me to bring you home early. You have a dental appointment this morning."

"Aw, gee," Tony said, shaking himself awake. "I wanted to stay here."

"Your mother can drop you off on the way back from the dentist, and you can finish painting the fence around the paddock. I'll be out in the fields, and if Dr. Weaver leaves any medicine, put it in that refrigerator here in the barn."

After the short trip to the Simpson farm and back, Nathan got on his tractor and headed toward the fields to cut alfalfa, hoping to avoid another encounter with Autumn until he stifled his emotions, but that was a mistake. One of his most memorable incidents with Autumn had occurred when he was cutting hay.

The summer day she'd returned home from college was seared in his memory. He'd been in the alfalfa field driving a team of Belgians hitched to a mower, when he'd seen her hurrying along the path to the pasture. She'd stopped when she reached the mower, and her eyes had brightened when he tipped back his hat so she could see his face. He'd heard about her homecoming, and he wondered if he'd see her. His pulse was racing, for he didn't suppose she would even remember him.

Her eyes had brightened. "Nathan?" she cried delightedly.

He'd grinned and stepped to the ground beside her.

"I didn't know you were working for Daddy."

"After Christmas I came back to Ohio and asked your dad for a job. He hired me the first of the year to take care of his young stock. I live in that little apartment over the tack room."

"Oh, I'm so glad. I remember you said you'd like to raise Belgians."

His dark face flushed, and embarrassed, he'd said, "That's only a dream. I don't suppose I'll ever reach it."

"You're at the right place to learn the trade. If anyone can teach you about draft horses, it's Daddy. I'm pleased to see you, Nathan. I've thought about you often this winter. I was never so happy to see anyone as I was when you showed up in the barn last Christmas Eve."

Surprised at her candor, Nathan had felt his face flushing. "I didn't do anything. You were the expert."

"But you were there! If you hadn't encouraged me, I might not have saved the foal."

They'd been standing on a high point providing an overview of the farm. Autumn had looked around in delight as she surveyed the four hundred acres of flat fields and slightly rolling hills bisected by Indian Creek and bounded with white board fences. She'd pulled off her sandals and run circles in the dark-green alfalfa hay while a slight breeze stirred her curly hair.

"Glad to be home, are you?" Nathan had said, grinning at her exuberance.

"Oh, yes! I'm going to the pasture to see Noel. How is she?"

"Looks like a fine filly to me. Bet you can't pick her out of the other foals."

"Of course I can! I've had her picture on my desk since Christmas. How much do you want to bet?"

"Just kidding!"

"No. I mean it. If I can pick Noel out of all the other foals, you buy me dinner. If I can't, I'll pay."

He shook his head. "I'm not betting."

"I've got to hurry. Mother insists that I be back in time for dinner. Can you go with me to the pasture?"

When he'd heard that Autumn was coming home for the summer, Nathan had made up his mind to avoid this girl who'd dominated his thoughts for months. Now that he'd seen her again, his good resolutions had dwindled. It was one thing to say he'd have nothing to do with Autumn when she was in Massachusetts. But seeing her in the flesh, her windblown red hair framing a smiling face, her luminous blue eyes smiling at him, all of his resolutions had disappeared as if he'd never made them.

Knowing it wasn't wise, Nathan had unhitched the reins and tied the horses to the fence, so they wouldn't stray while he was gone. "I only have another hour's work, so I can spare a few minutes."

"What else have you been doing since I saw you?" Autumn asked as they walked side by side.

"I've been taking night classes at OSU's agricultural college, where I've learned you need a lot of head knowledge, as well as experience and money to become a farmer. Uncle Matthew is helping me.''

Nathan's father, a half brother of Matthew Holland, had never been a good provider, and Nathan had grown up in poverty. His father resented Matthew's affluence and distanced himself from his brother, but after the death of Nathan's father, Matthew had helped his sister-in-law and her three boys.

''So, you still think you'd like to be a farmer? That episode at Christmas didn't discourage you?''

Nathan had shaken his head, but didn't answer. He couldn't think dispassionately about anything that had happened at their first meeting.

When they'd reached the pasture, Autumn clapped her hands when she saw the ten red foals grazing. ''Aren't they beautiful?''

''I think so.'' Nathan had unlatched the fence, and ten sorrel heads lifted expectantly. Nathan took a halter from a fence post, and they entered the pasture and walked slowly toward the young animals, whose legs seemed much too long in proportion to their graceful slender bodies. Their chestnut coats gleamed like burnished copper, and a breeze ruffled the white manes.

''They're used to me,'' Nathan had said, ''so I can usually catch them. They've only been weaned for a few weeks, but I've been breaking them to the halter all winter. Pick out Noel, and I'll put a halter on her.''

Autumn walked slowly among the foals and looked at all of them carefully before she stopped in front of one and ran her hand over the white strip on its face. ''That's Noel,'' she said, and Nathan grinned, walked to the filly and put the halter around her neck.

''How did you know?''

''Instinct, maybe. Remember I've grown up with

Belgian colts, but mostly, because I found that red star in the middle of her forehead. That's the clue I looked for.''

Noel had tossed her head, but she'd quieted when Autumn's hands caressed her neck and shoulders. ''Oh, she's wonderful. Do you think I have time to train her for showing at the state fair in August?''

''I don't have a clue, but your dad will know.''

''But I'm not sure he'll agree to let me show Noel. He might, if Mother doesn't interfere.'' Autumn had given the filly another hug when they left the pasture.

Before they parted in the hay field, Autumn had said, ''Don't forget, you lost the bet.''

Wanting desperately to have a date with her, he'd shaken his head. ''I'm sorry, Autumn. I think your father is pleased with my work at Indian Creek Farm, but he wouldn't approve if I took you out for dinner. A few months ago, one of the workers invited your sister to go to a church meeting, and Mr. Weaver fired him immediately.''

''I'm old enough to choose my own friends. I like you.''

Nathan's heart had leaped at her words, but trying to control the tremor in his voice, he said patiently, ''You don't understand. Just because you and I met under unusual circumstances doesn't mean we can be friends.''

''We will, if I have anything to say about it.''

''Give me a break, Autumn. I need this job. I want to work here, so don't get me in trouble with the boss.''

When he stepped back on the mower, she'd said, ''I can handle Daddy.''

Famous last words! Nathan thought as he remembered what had happened on the day Landon Weaver had fired him.

Chapter Four

The clinic resembled most medical doctors' offices. A small waiting room contained several chairs, and magazine racks were filled with periodicals for adults as well as magazines to interest children. A small wooden desk provided a place for Miss Olive to serve as Ray's receptionist.

The office contained modern computer equipment with Ray's accounts entered into the system. The records were up-to-date, and Trina and Autumn had little trouble understanding how he operated his clinic. Two surgery rooms, an X-ray room, a half-dozen cages and several runways provided good facilities.

The morning passed quickly as they pumped the stomach of a cat that had helped itself to a pizza laced with hot peppers, gave several dogs a series of shots, and treated a large brown rabbit for ear mites.

Dolly had been an interested bystander in the surgery rooms, but with her first question, Trina said sternly, "You may watch as long as you stay out of our way and keep quiet. Get up on that stool and stop talking."

"And I thought *going* to vet school was hard," Trina complained when they went into the kitchen for the hot lunch Olive had prepared.

"Welcome to the *real* world, Trina," Autumn said as she sat down. "I followed Ray around long enough when I was a kid to know that a vet doesn't have an easy job, but I can't think of anything I'd rather be doing."

Dolly was placing plates and cutlery on the table. "Can I ask questions now, Aunt Trina?" she asked.

Trina laughed. "I suppose so. I'm sorry I was cross with you, but I was nervous because it was our first day on the job. I didn't want to make any mistakes."

"Oh, that's all right. Why do cats and dogs need shots? You treated those animals just like they were real people, taking X-rays and stuff."

"Animals need shots to make them well, or keep them healthy, the same as you do," Trina said. "I won't tell you all the names, for you wouldn't remember them anyway, but animals can have the same kind of diseases humans do—viruses, hepatitis, heart trouble, Lyme disease and lots of other things."

"Gee!" Dolly said, her expressive gray eyes sparkling.

"I noticed Ray has kept up with the latest in medical equipment," Autumn said to Olive. "He has everything our professors recommended that we should buy when we started out on our own."

Pleased, Olive said, "He's always interested in the latest cures and supplies. The reason he took this long tour is to study diseases and medical procedures in other countries. But he has more work than he can handle." Looking keenly at Autumn, she said, "He needs another vet, so he won't have to be on call all the time. Why don't you and Trina stay on when he gets back? Ray would like to semiretire, and all of you could make a good living here."

Olive had always fussed like a mother hen over her bachelor brother, and Autumn figured this idea of semiretirement was more her idea than Ray's. Still, if problems of the past could be erased, it would be nice to settle down in Greensboro, especially now that Nathan was living in the county.

But would she be able to receive Nathan's forgiveness and win his love? Did she even want his love now? Was that a pipe dream of the past? Would her parents forgive her and welcome her into the family circle again? Until she knew the answer to those questions, Autumn wasn't making any promises.

"Thanks, Miss Olive," Trina said, "but I'm engaged to a great guy who has a few more months of veterinarian training. When he's licensed, we plan to take over his father's practice in St. Louis. It sounds like a good opportunity for Autumn, though," Trina said with a meaningful glance at her friend.

"We'll wait and see how these two months turn out."

Slumping in her chair to rest a bit, Autumn jumped when frantic pounding sounded at the back door.

"Help! Help!" a youthful voice yelled.

Autumn rushed out on the porch.

A teenage boy stood on the back step. Tears glistened in his eyes and he swiped them away.

"Flossie's got a broken leg. She's in the truck."

Autumn opened the screen door, calling, "Come to

the clinic when you can, Trina.'' The boy ran down the sidewalk, and Autumn's long-legged stride kept up with him.

A girl, younger than the boy, sat in the back of a pickup holding a bleating goat in her arms.

Autumn took the struggling goat from the girl, who jumped out of the truck and ran beside Autumn. The boy sprinted ahead to open the door, and Autumn carried the animal inside the clinic. The goat's left foreleg dangled helplessly.

''What happened?'' Autumn asked.

''A mean ole' dog jumped on her,'' the little girl said, her lips quivering.

''Don't worry,'' Autumn said. ''Flossie will be as good as new in a few weeks.''

Trina, with Dolly tagging at her heels, came into the surgery and prepared to tranquilize the goat. The three children crowded close to the operating table.

''Hey! We can't have this,'' Trina said. ''Dolly, you go back in the house.''

A hefty woman, who'd been driving the pickup, came into the waiting room. Without saying a word, she gestured to her children and they scuttled out of the surgery. With another quick look at the goat, Dolly ran out too, and Trina closed the door.

While Autumn scrubbed her hands and arms, Trina put a mask over Flossie's nose and slowly sedated her until she was as limp as a rag. Autumn carried her to the X-ray room to determine the extent of the break. Fortunately, the bone hadn't punctured the skin, so Autumn straightened the leg and encased it in a Thomas splint. The goat was still sedated when she called the family in. The little girl patted the goat's head.

"Flossie, you'll be all right," she crooned.

The woman followed her children and held out her hand to Autumn. "I'm Sandy Simpson, and my kids are Tony and Debbie. Welcome to Greensboro."

"Tony, you look familiar," Autumn said.

"I work for Mr. Holland. I saw you at his farm last night."

"Oh, yes. I didn't get a good look at you in the darkness." She turned back to Sandy. "Thanks for the welcome, but actually, I'm a native of this area. I'm Autumn Weaver. This is my associate, Trina Jackson."

"Weaver, as in Weavers of Indian Creek Farm?" Sandy asked, amazement mirrored on her round face.

"Yes, but I've been gone for several years," Autumn said evenly. No doubt she'd be answering that question often in the next two months.

"Stop by our farm for a visit when you're out that way," Sandy said. "We live a few miles north of Woodbeck Farm. We run a few cattle, but our major interest is horses. We have three Thoroughbreds now, but we don't intend to buy any more until we see how we make out with them."

Sandy wrote a check for their services.

"In case there might be complications," Autumn explained, "I'd like to see Flossie again tomorrow morning. The splint will need to stay on a few weeks, but check a couple of times each day above the splint for swelling or dampness. Also, feel the foot to make sure it's warm, which is an indication of normal circulation."

"Can Flossie walk now?" the boy questioned.

"Sure," Trina said.

Still a bit woozy, Flossie staggered when Autumn

set her on the floor, but she wobbled out of the building to the delight of her happy family.

A bemused expression on her face, Autumn said,
"That's the reason I wanted to become a vet. I like to
bring happiness to people, especially children."

"But we can't heal all their pets, and that's going
to hurt," Trina replied.

Leaving Trina to handle the office work, Autumn
made calls to two dairy farms where some cows were
in the early stages of grass tetany, but the cases
weren't as severe as Nathan's cow had been. By late
afternoon, as she turned into the driveway of Woodbeck Farm, every nerve in her body was twanging at
the thought of seeing Nathan again.

Nathan's home, a pre-Civil War structure named
Woodbeck after the Holland family's ancestral home
in England, had been completely renovated during the
lifetime of his grandfather. The brick walls had been
painted white and modern accommodations added several years ago. At one time, it had rivaled the Weaver
farmhouse for beauty, a fact that Clara refused to acknowledge. Since Matt Holland had been a bachelor,
he hadn't kept the house nor grounds in tiptop shape,
but the two-story building with huge chimneys at each
end and a comfortable front veranda the width of the
house was still an architectural masterpiece.

Matt had spared no expense on his red wooden
barns and utility buildings, and Nathan had followed
his example. Autumn's heart swelled when she saw
the newly painted buildings and the herd of Angus
cattle grazing in a nearby pasture. It seemed like a
miracle that Nathan's youthful dreams had been ful-
filled.

Tony Simpson sauntered off the back porch.

"Mr. Holland's gone," he said. "He said to tell you the cow's still in the stall. You can check her and leave your bill with me. He'll mail you a check."

Autumn felt as if she'd been drenched in a bucket of ice water. Was Nathan avoiding her? she wondered. A red pickup was parked in front of the house so he must be working on the farm. She scanned the fields around the house, but she didn't see him.

Since their chance meeting last night had been amicable, she'd hoped they could become friends and maybe move from friendship to a more intimate relationship. She didn't ask the boy where Nathan had gone. The events of the past few years had been humbling, but she still had a touch of the Weaver pride.

"How's Flossie doing?" she asked to break the silence.

"Okay," Tony said. "We've got her in a pen so she won't move around too much and hurt herself. "

The cow's condition was vastly improved, but Autumn gave her another injection of magnesium oxide and handed the bottle to Tony.

"Tell Mr. Holland to give her the rest of this bottle in daily injections. He can turn her out to pasture in a week. The weather forecast is for dry, hot weather over the next few days, so that should eliminate conditions that cause grass tetany. Mr. Holland can telephone if he needs any more help."

On her way back to Greensboro, Autumn drove by Indian Creek Farm. Fences that had once been snow-white were now a dingy gray. A dozen Belgian mares grazed in a pasture near the road. When Autumn slowed the truck, they lifted their heads, but she couldn't tell if Noel was among them. The house was

partially hidden by the maple trees that were notice-
ably larger than they had been the last time she'd seen
them. Autumn paused at the driveway, wanting desperately to go home, but after several minutes, she
continued toward Greensboro.

Not knowing what time Autumn would come to
Woodbeck Farm, Nathan had left in early morning to
work on the far side of Indian Creek. The ground was
too wet for cultivating, so he spent the day repairing
fence, a job he detested and normally put off as long
as he could. Today, he looked forward to the tedious
work as an excuse to be away from the farm buildings
when Autumn came.

Nathan had learned to live without Autumn, and he
didn't want her to disrupt his life again. He'd been
convinced she would never return to Greensboro, or
he wouldn't have settled here. He could have sold
Woodbeck Farm and bought a comparable farm in another location where the memory of Autumn wouldn't
eat at him like a canker. After he took possession of
his uncle's farm, he could never pass Indian Creek
Farm without remembering Autumn. On those days,
he had often wished he could see her again, believing
that the person she'd become after eight years
wouldn't appeal to him at all. Now, he groaned at the
thought. In spite of the sadness that marked her expression, the bewitching, impulsive teenager who'd
captured his heart had turned into a stunning, enig-
matic beauty. To his dismay, he'd learned he was still
susceptible to her allure.

To avoid recalling the things he admired about Autumn, he deliberately thought of the things he resented
about her. She'd caused him to lose his job at Indian

Creek Farm and his good standing in the community, for the neighbors had jumped to the wrong conclusions about why Landon Weaver had fired him. Now it annoyed him even more to realize that the resentment he'd harbored for years disappeared when he had looked up and saw her kneeling beside him in the muddy pasture field. He had to avoid her. He wouldn't trust Autumn with his heart again.

Chapter Five

"I'm taking Dolly to Sunday school tomorrow morning," Trina said on Saturday evening as they lingered at the supper table, sipping iced tea. "Want to come with us?"

"No, thanks," Autumn said, "someone has to be on call, and I shouldn't take my beeper to church."

"Miss Olive goes to eight o'clock service at her church," Trina continued, "and she says she'll be home in time to answer the phone. If an emergency comes up, she can reach us by telephone at the church."

"What church? Where are you going?"

"Community Chapel. It's a new congregation on the east side of town. Sandy Simpson told me about it and invited us to attend. She said it's mostly younger couples who've moved into the region without any family ties here. I think you should go."

Autumn took her iced tea and sauntered out on the back porch and sat in a rocking chair. Trina followed and leaned against the porch railing.

"What's bothering you, Autumn? You were animated and happy when we first got here. What's wrong?"

"The same old thing that's plagued me since you've known me. I wonder sometimes how you ever became my friend. You're an upbeat person, always with an optimistic outlook on life. We've been here four days, and my parents haven't made any overtures. And I've hoped that Nathan would telephone or stop by. He could have come in to pay his bill, but instead we got a check in the mail today for that vet call."

"The Bible has a lot to say about forgiveness. Sometimes it's the person who's been wronged that has to make the first move."

"I asked Nathan to forgive me, and he brushed my apology aside. And making the first move was what got me in wrong with Nathan and my parents before."

"I know you think you're the one who was wrong, but your parents are as much to blame as you are. They had no reason to disown you and forbid you to come home."

"I disappointed them."

"What children haven't disappointed their parents in some way?" Trina argued. "Did you disappoint Nathan, too?"

"That's a different matter. I pursued him when he tried to get me to stop. Right from the first, I think the attraction was mostly on my side," Autumn reminisced. "I was never sure what he thought about me. So don't blame Nathan. He didn't promise me anything, I expected too much. It's little wonder he's avoiding me."

Autumn drained the rest of her tea and stretched her long legs. "Yes, I'll go to church with you in the morning," she said. "As weak as my faith is, I need some spiritual nurturing."

Trina laid an arm over Autumn's shoulders. "I'm sorry, Autumn. I know it's hard to give up a dream. I've prayed that you'd get to meet Nathan again, but perhaps that was the wrong thing to ask for."

Autumn shook her head. "No. I'm thankful I know where he is and how he's getting along. That's important to me, no matter how our association turns out."

Community Chapel stood near a new housing development. Autumn thought the congregation was mostly drawn from that area, for she didn't recognize anyone as they walked into the crowded foyer of the metal building. An overweight, blondish, brown-eyed man came forward to greet them with a cordial smile and a warm handshake.

"I'm Elwood Donahue, pastor of the church. Welcome to our fellowship." He asked for their names and Dolly's age.

"Our classes are about to begin." He called a child, and Autumn recognized the girl as the one who'd brought the wounded goat to the clinic. "Debbie, take Dolly to class with you, please. Autumn, if you and Trina will come with me, I'll show you to the Berean classroom and introduce you to the teacher. Our worship service is at eleven," he said as he walked beside them down the hallway.

"An interesting name for the class," Trina said, chatting with the pastor in the easy way she had.

"The members organized the class for the specific purpose of searching the Scriptures to learn the way to abundant Christian living. We were fortunate to find a good teacher for the group.''

He paused at a door displaying a poster, on which a Scripture verse was printed in calligraphy.

''The purpose of the class is indicated in this biblical passage,'' Elwood said, reading the words, '''Now the Bereans were of more noble character than the Thessalonians, for they received the message with great eagerness and examined the Scriptures every day to see if what Paul said was true.'''

''This should be an interesting class,'' Trina said. ''I'm looking forward to it.''

Elwood motioned them into a well-lit room where several people stood talking. ''Let me have your attention, folks,'' he said, ''we have guests this morning. Make them welcome.'' He tapped a man on the shoulder.

''Nathan, Trina Jackson and Autumn Weaver have come to worship with us. They've taken over for Doc Wheeler while he's abroad.'' To Autumn and Trina, he explained, ''Nathan will be your teacher.''

Nathan wheeled around, and a sudden hush fell over the room as he and Autumn locked eyes, tense in their concentration on each other. Autumn was suddenly dizzy, and she closed her eyes. She'd never fainted in her life. These unexpected meetings with Nathan were tearing her apart. What if she dropped at Nathan's feet?

It hadn't entered Nathan's mind that he would see Autumn this morning. What had brought her to church today? To see him? His pulse quickened at the thought.

But how could he teach a Bible lesson with her blue

eyes watching his every move? After such a long time, why did the Weavers still intimidate him?

A buzzer sounded in the hall, and Nathan shook his head as if to clear the fog away. "Won't all of you be seated? It's time to start. We're pleased to have visitors this morning," he added with an effort.

Nathan's face flushed when he took his place behind the podium. His fingers fumbled through the pages of his Bible.

God, what can I do? Why are You subjecting me to this torture? I'm trying to serve You, to be a witness for You in this community. I can't make a fool of myself before these people. Help me!

Keenly aware of Nathan's agitation, and knowing she was the cause of it, Autumn muttered, "I'm going to leave."

"No," Trina whispered as she slid into a chair on the back row.

"Did you know Nathan attended this church?" Autumn demanded accusingly.

"No. No. I had no idea," Trina protested. She clutched Autumn's arm and pulled her into a chair. "If you leave, that would only make it worse. Tough it out."

Autumn did as Trina commanded, but she couldn't remember when she'd spent a more miserable hour. Her body was rigid, and she stared at her hands where veins bulged from a racing pulse. And Nathan was so uncomfortable her heart ached for him. She sensed that ordinarily he would be an effective teacher, but he hardly looked up as he read the text almost word by word from the lesson book, often faltering on the words.

Several people seated in front of her glanced at one

another in amazement, affirming her belief that Nathan's current behavior wasn't natural. The lesson subject itself was enough to distress Nathan, as the Scriptural text was taken from the Model Prayer from the book of Luke. When he read the words, "Forgive us our sins, for we also forgive everyone who sins against us," Nathan's face paled even more. His voice was barely audible when he stumbled over the next words, "and lead us not into temptation."

Perspiration drenched his face when he finally sat down on a chair behind the podium, and the president of the class stood up. Autumn recognized the woman as Sandy Simpson, the mother of the two children who owned Flossie, the pet goat.

"We need to make final plans for our picnic next Saturday afternoon," Sandy stated. "Nathan has graciously invited us to picnic in the hickory nut grove on his farm. Burgers and buns will be provided from our class treasury, but it's up to us to bring the rest of the food. Plan to arrive early and stay until evening. We'll eat around half-past four."

Sandy asked for a show of hands of those who planned to attend the picnic, suggested they should sign a sheet on the bulletin board indicating the food they'd contribute, then closed the session with a prayer. She made a beeline for Trina and Autumn as soon as she said, "Amen."

"You must come to the picnic Saturday," Sandy said. "That will give us an opportunity to get better acquainted." Looking at Autumn, she said, "Families are invited, too, so you can bring your daughter."

"Daughter?" Autumn looked from Sandy to Trina, wondering what the woman meant.

"Dolly is your daughter, isn't she?"

"Of course not," Autumn answered, more sharply than she should have.

"Forgive me. I was misinformed."

"Dolly's name is Rossini. She's my niece," Trina said.

"Oh, I see," Sandy said, with a skeptical look at Autumn. "You'll come to the picnic?"

Autumn didn't answer, and Trina said, "We'll try, if our work schedule isn't too heavy. We're finding out that we've taken up a time-consuming profession."

Dolly joined them in the foyer and they went into the sanctuary together. Autumn looked keenly at the child, wondering who'd started the rumor that Dolly was her daughter. The gray-eyed girl with brown hair didn't resemble the Weavers at all, but with a start, Autumn realized that Dolly's features were similar to Nathan's.

Just what I need, she thought morosely, to have such a story circulating. What had Nathan said that morning at the farm? "It took me months to convince people that you and I hadn't been living together."

Would Dolly's resemblance to Nathan cause him any embarrassment?

During the informal service, Autumn momentarily forgot the miserable hour she'd spent in Nathan's class. Elwood Donahue wasn't a dynamic speaker, but his message on commitment was simple and easy to understand. Lacking a deep understanding of the Bible, Elwood's straightforward explanation of the Scripture passage filled Autumn's need to have the Gospel presented simply, and soothed her spirit temporarily.

Nathan chose a pew behind Autumn, and he was

vividly conscious of her presence. Why wouldn't he be, with her red head catching the lights from the windows? Had Autumn deliberately come to church to embarrass him? Was she still pursuing him as she'd done when she was a girl?

God, he thought during the pastoral prayer, *why do You keep bringing us together? Has she changed from the willful, spoiled girl who almost ruined my life? Can I trust her again?*

He'd resolved to avoid Autumn, but how could he when they attended the same church? Was it unchristian of him to keep thinking of the past? Was he the one who'd been wrong to leave without giving her the opportunity to explain? But after Autumn had run out of the horse barn eight years ago, her father said, "Autumn is going to marry Dr. Lowe. Can't you have the decency to leave her alone? When I told you to leave, I meant leave this area. You'll be nothing but a thorn in the flesh of our whole family if you stay here. There's already a lot of gossip about you and Autumn seeing each other while I've been gone."

Even though Autumn had protested that she'd never intended to marry Dr. Lowe, he'd wondered if she was telling the truth. But with Landon's ultimatum, he had no choice except to leave. The Weavers had enough influence to ruin him in the community if they wanted to. When he'd left Greensboro, he supposed his brief association with Autumn was over. Now their paths had crossed again, Autumn looked as if she was unhappy. Had she really cared for him? Did she still care for him? How could he find out?

As Nathan drove home from church, his emotions were tumultuous. One minute, the desire to be with Autumn was so overpowering that he almost returned to Greensboro to talk with her. The next minute he dreaded the thought of seeing her again, and actually considered offering the farm for sale and leaving the country.

Sandy Simpson invited Dolly to spend the afternoon at her house to play with her daughter. As Autumn and Trina drove home alone, Autumn said, "I'll have to find another place to worship."

"I don't know why you should."

"It's obvious that my presence made Nathan uncomfortable, and I was miserable."

"I agree it was an awkward moment, but you'll both adjust to the situation. If not, I suppose you could skip Sunday school and come for the worship service. You need to hear the Word of God proclaimed from the pulpit."

"But if I do that, I might drive Nathan away. He made no effort to speak with me after the morning service. I saw him hurrying to his truck as if he wanted to avoid me."

"You're creating problems when there aren't any. Maybe he was in a hurry to check on his livestock."

As she turned into the driveway at the Wheeler home, Autumn cast an oblique glance at Trina. "What did you make of Sandy's comment that Dolly is my daughter?"

Trina replied with a bubbling laugh. "When I first saw Nathan, I knew he reminded me of someone, but I didn't have a clue until Sandy came up with that remark." She laughed again. "If I didn't know Dolly got her physical features from her Italian father, and that my sister has never laid eyes on Nathan, I could believe that Dolly was his daughter."

"It's a coincidence, but one that might become irritating. I imagine my reputation in Greensboro is already bad enough, because I made no secret of how much I liked Nathan. Since no one knew why I'd run away, people may have thought the worst. I suppose one more suspicion won't matter to me, but I don't want to tarnish Nathan's image. He and I know very well that it was impossible for me to bear his child, but how can we prove it to others?"

"You can't. It would be helpful if Dolly looked like our side of the family, but unfortunately, she doesn't. If I were you, I'd ignore the situation."

"I guess I'll have to."

Chapter Six

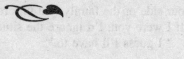

"No emergency calls." Miss Olive met them at the door with the news and a wide grin. "Maybe this can really be a day of rest for you."

"Good!" Trina said. "That will give me time to unpack all of my clothes and sort out my laundry."

Autumn was too restless to stay in the house all afternoon, and she said to Trina, "If you're going to be here in case an emergency does come up, do you mind if I leave? I want to drive around and see what's changed in the county since I left."

"Go ahead," Trina insisted.

"I'll keep my phone handy if you need me."

"Don't leave until you've eaten," Olive said. "I've got chicken and dumplings, and if I remember, you always liked them."

"Sure do. I have no intention of missing one of your meals unless I have to."

"Miss Olive, does Ray still keep his fishing rods in the garage?" Autumn asked as she got up from the table. "I haven't gone fishing since Ray and I used to fish in Indian Creek. We were fishing the day I told him I wanted to be a veterinarian, and he encouraged me to pursue it as a career."

"He always said you had the makings of a vet," Olive said. "I'm sure you'll find what you want in the garage."

While Autumn picked up some fishing gear and stashed it in the truck, she recalled that Ray was one of the few people who knew how much she was interested in Nathan. They'd been fishing that day, too—one of those unhappy summer days when her parents had decided it was time she stopped working on the farm to follow more ladylike pursuits.

Soon after Autumn had arrived home from her first year in college, Landon and Clara had gone away for two weeks, leaving Autumn and Summer in the care of their housekeeper, Mrs. Hayes. During that time, Nathan and Autumn had spent every day together, training Noel, working in the fields, bringing the young stock in from the pasture early in the morning.

As long as Autumn was in by ten o'clock, when Mrs. Hayes wanted to go to bed, the housekeeper didn't pay much attention to what she was doing. Autumn and Nathan often went fishing at a spot where Indian Creek flowed from the Weaver property onto Woodbeck Farm. Several times they drove in Nathan's old truck to Jimmy's Drive-in, a favorite stopping place for young people. Summer had warned Autumn that the neighbors were talking about that young Weaver girl who was crazy about one of Landon's farmhands. Summer worried that their parents would find out about how much time Autumn was spending with Nathan, but Autumn was headstrong.

The parental axe fell the day Landon and Clara returned. Landon chose a punishment that he knew would hurt Autumn the most. Early that morning when she started toward the barn to work with Noel, Landon stopped her on the back veranda.

"I've hired Jeff Smith to train our colts, and I don't want you interfering with his work. Jeff has had lots of experience on his father's horse farm in Kentucky."

"But, Daddy," Autumn had protested. "Noel is mine, and I'm getting along great with her. I think she'll be ready for competition in the Ohio State Fair."

"That decision will be up to Jeff and me. Your mother says its time for you to stay out of the barns, and I agree with her."

Autumn remembered she'd stamped her foot at her father—a most unwise thing to do. "No! I'm like you, Daddy. Raising Belgian horses is in my blood. And I might as well tell you now, I'm not going back East to college this fall, either. I want to stay here and train Noel."

For a moment Autumn thought Landon had wavered, but in a dogmatic tone she'd heard him use often, but never on her, Landon said, "You will do as I say. Furthermore, I won't have you ruining your chances of a good future by dallying around Nathan Holland. The boy's a good worker, but he has no prospects. I've told him to stay away from you. If he doesn't, I'll fire him and see to it that he doesn't get another job in this community."

She knew the finality in her father's voice, and Autumn hadn't argued anymore. Knowing she wouldn't find any sympathy from her mother, and that she shouldn't involve Summer in her problems, Autumn had gotten in her white convertible and driven into Greensboro. Ray was climbing into his pickup when she parked beside the animal clinic.

"Hi. Can I come along, Ray?"

"Sure. I've got one stop to make and then I'm going fishing. Go in the garage and get yourself a rod."

They'd spent several hours vaccinating a dairy herd that had contacted Leptospirosis, a contagious bacterial disease that caused fever, weakness, anemia and lowered milk production.

Afterward, they'd driven to a popular fishing hole in Indian Creek. Leaning against trees, their poles dangling in the water, Ray had said, "Thanks for your help, Autumn. Do you want a job helping me this summer?"

"I thought I had a job breaking and training my filly for the state fair."

"No reason you can't. She looks like a blue ribbon winner to me."

Autumn had always shared her troubles with Ray, so she'd said, "Mother and Daddy have other plans for me. Daddy has hired a trainer for the young stock, and I've been ordered to stay out of the barns."

Ray whistled and his eyes twinkled. "No wonder you're upset."

"Nathan Holland's a good hand with horses. I don't know why Daddy hired someone else."

"I'd heard you'd gotten acquainted with Nathan."

Autumn had darted a quick look at Ray, but she couldn't tell from his expression whether he approved or disapproved of her friendship with Nathan.

"What do you think of him?"

"I've only seen Nathan a few times," Ray had said,

carefully choosing his words. "He's interested in horses. He's asked a lot of questions about my work."

"He wants to own a farm."

"Quite an ambition for a poor man. In this day and age, with the high cost of land, machinery and livestock, there's no way a man can make a success of farming unless he has money for an initial investment. Unless his uncle helps him, Nathan wouldn't have a chance," Ray added, and Autumn had wondered if his words were a warning.

They left the creek without any fish, but the hour in Ray's presence had soothed Autumn's anger. As they neared Greensboro, Ray said, "You've been a big help today. What's happened to your dream of becoming a vet?"

"Smothered," Autumn said bitterly. "I'm not surprised that Mother opposes me, but I'd have thought Daddy would understand. When I told him I wanted to go to veterinarian school, he put his foot down. 'No daughter of mine is going to make her living that way'," Autumn had said in perfect imitation of Landon's dogmatic tones.

Ray had chuckled sympathetically. "That's too bad. Lots of women choose to become vets now, and you can be a vet without doing the dirty work we did today. Many veterinarians confine their practices to small animals."

"Don't you think I can handle livestock?" Autumn had demanded.

"Of course you can," Wheeler soothed. "And don't give up yet. Landon may change his mind. He's always let you do what you wanted to."

Autumn shook her head. "Not this time."

Ray had glanced at her sympathetically as he drove his pickup into the garage. "Nathan Holland?"

Autumn hadn't answered him, but when he squeezed her hand, she knew he'd guessed her secret.

Physically satisfied with the big lunch Olive had provided, but still fretting over her encounter with Nathan at church, Autumn crisscrossed the county on various rural roads, happy to find out that industry hadn't swallowed up farmland in this area as it had done in many other states. She carefully avoided the road that led to Woodbeck Farm and her former home.

She phoned the clinic. When Miss Olive reported it was still a quiet afternoon, Autumn turned onto a gravel road, her destination a deep fishing hole in Indian Creek where it divided her father's farm and Nathan's property. She would have to walk across Weaver land to get to the creek, but hopefully her father wouldn't know she was there. She parked her car beside the road, took the tackle box and rod and plunged downhill toward the stream. She was hidden from view in a short time by trees and thick underbrush.

Autumn soon discovered that a return to this spot didn't bring her peace of mind. She'd spent too many happy times here with Nathan. She didn't even bother to prepare the rod for fishing. She stood looking into the clear water. Tiny minnows wiggled in the shallow water that flowed slowly over the gravel bed toward the deeper hole. Autumn picked up a few pieces of gravel, pitched them into the water and watched the ripples spread. Hearing a sound behind her, she whirled quickly.

Nathan was leaning against a tree watching her.

"Oh, hello," she said, "you caught me trespassing. I thought it was Daddy."

"Let's hope he doesn't catch either one of us." Smiling, he walked toward her.

"You still like to fish, huh?"

"I haven't done much of it lately." Noticing his empty hands, she said, "You aren't fishing today?"

How could he explain that he'd been compelled to come because he sensed he would find her here? "No. Sometimes I walk around the farm on Sunday afternoons, mostly thanking God for what I have. I saw you and decided to join you. Go ahead and fish if you want to."

He sat on the ground and leaned against a maple tree. In jeans and a knit shirt, he looked so much different than he had this morning at church when he'd been dressed in a gray suit and a blue knit shirt. He'd seemed older then, like a stranger to Autumn, but now as he relaxed, he was more like the youth she'd known.

"I don't really care whether I fish or not," Autumn said, sitting beside him, her legs crossed. "I wanted to get off by myself for a bit. I've been driving around to see what's changed. I'm happy the farms haven't been sold to developers."

"Did you go by your dad's place?"

She shook her head. "Not today, but I did drive by on the highway a couple of days ago. I can't bring myself to go to the house. Maybe he'll need a vet someday and will call for me. It isn't easy to go somewhere when you think you're not welcome. I even felt guilty walking across a corner of his farm to get to the creek."

Nathan picked up a stick and pitched it into the

creek. They laughed when a fish, looking for a hand-out, dived toward the stick.

"I'm happy you came to church this morning."

"You didn't act like it. Sandy Simpson had invited us, and I didn't know you went to that church. I wasn't following you."

"You surprised me, the past flooded my mind and I just couldn't throw it off. I acted very foolish."

"I'm sorry I embarrassed you." Why was she always apologizing to Nathan?

"That's okay. It's my problem, not yours. This is the first class I've taught, and I don't have much confidence in my teaching ability. I was afraid I wouldn't do a good job. I didn't want you to be ashamed of me."

"I wasn't. But I won't come again. I don't want to upset you."

"Please don't stay away. I'll be expecting you the next time. If you're going to be here most of the summer, we can't avoid each other. Not that I want to avoid you," he added hurriedly.

"Then I'll continue to come. I need all the Bible instruction I can get. I didn't learn anything about Christianity at home."

"That's another way we differ," he said, as though he kept a running tally of their differences rather than what they had in common. "My mother didn't have many material possessions to give me, but she always took my two brothers and me to church. I could recite Bible verses before I knew my ABCs. Prayer, Bible reading and church attendance became a way of life for me, but I'd never tried to teach until I went to Community Chapel."

Small white flowers grew all around them. While

they talked, Nathan carefully picked several of the biggest blossoms, fashioned them into a small bouquet and tied them together with a small vine.

"Daddy didn't work on Sunday, but it was a day of rest to him rather than a day to worship. It's strange how different our childhoods were. When I was growing up, I used to compare myself with other kids in the neighborhood and consider how lucky I was. Now I'm not so sure. My parents may have neglected giving me what I needed the most."

Grinning, Nathan threw a twig in her direction, and she caught it. "While I always wondered what it would be like to be born with a silver spoon in my mouth."

She made a face at him and pitched the twig back toward him, but her heart rejoiced. This was the kind of tomfoolery they had enjoyed during the two weeks they'd spent so much time together. "A silver spoon in your mouth might be all right when you're born. It can become mighty burdensome when you're an adult."

He handed her the bouquet. She thanked him, pulled a white stretchy band from her pocket and fastened the white flowers on her hair. They spent an hour lounging on the creek's bank bantering each other without referring to the times they'd shared there in the past. But she knew those days were as prominent in Nathan's mind as they were in hers when he said, "Jimmy's Drive-In is still operating. How'd you like to drive there for a hot dog and some fries?"

She smiled, and her eyes glowed with pleasure. "I'd like it very much, Nathan."

He got up and dusted the dead leaves off the seat of his pants. He held out his hand and lifted Autumn upward until she stood close beside him. What would she do if he kissed her? Nathan wondered. He bent slightly toward her until he could feel her soft breath on his face. But almost as if Landon Weaver was watching them, he remembered the last time he'd kissed her. He straightened. Autumn's eyes registered disappointment.

"You drive over to the farm," he said huskily, "and I'll cut through the woods and meet you at the house. Okay?"

She picked up the tackle box and fishing rod. "I'll be along soon."

Autumn's feet had been heavy as she'd walked the path to the creek, now she felt like running back to the truck. He hadn't forgotten! Whatever had been between them in the past hadn't completely died. Don't push him this time, she warned herself. Let him make the advances. But she only had two months! Before she got to the truck, Autumn knelt beside the path.

God, when I met Nathan, I didn't know You. You know my heart, so You're aware that those two fun weeks Nathan and I enjoyed together meant more than anything that's ever happened to me. He understood me more than anyone ever had. He encouraged me to be a vet. Made me feel like I was an individual, rather than just one of the Weaver daughters. Maybe I was drawn to him because I needed a big brother. Maybe it was something more powerful than that. I don't know. Now I've trusted my life to Your providence. If it's Your will for us to be together, let it happen this summer. If it's not Your will, help me to accept it, so I won't spend the rest of my life longing for something I shouldn't have. Amen.

Many times when Autumn prayed, she wasn't sure

that God even heard her. Today, she got off her knees confident that He had heard and would answer in His own way. She hadn't learned Bible verses when she was a child as Nathan had, but she had committed a few to memory. One came to her now. "This is the assurance we have in approaching God: that if we ask anything according to His will, He hears us. And if we know that He hears us, whatever we ask, we know that we have what we asked of Him."

It might still be an uphill battle, but Autumn was convinced that if it was God's will, she'd have what she wanted. Eight years ago, she'd wanted Nathan regardless of the consequences. But the years had taught her one important lesson. She couldn't be happy if she rebelled against God's will for her life.

Chapter Seven

Nathan waited for her when she arrived at his farm and parked her car under a large oak tree at the edge of the driveway. He opened the door of his truck, gave her a hand up, and she scooted under the steering wheel, staying in the middle of the seat so their shoulders touched. Mentally, they were as close as they used to be. She wanted to sense his physical presence, too.

Nathan started the engine of his late-model truck. When they'd dated before, they'd gone in his old pickup, and she'd left her luxury car at home. Now she was the one with the old car. It pleased her that he had a better vehicle than she did.

A half-hour later they pulled into the little drive-in that seemed dingier than it had the last time they'd been there together. "Do you want to go inside?" Nathan asked.

"Let's order and eat in the truck. That would seem more like old times."

"What do you want on your hot dog? Meat sauce and slaw as always?"

"Don't forget a little bit of onion. That way, I won't notice all those onions you eat."

He grinned and didn't even ask what else she wanted. He pulled up to the microphone and gave the order. "Two hot dogs. One with meat sauce, slaw and a few pieces of onion. Put a lot of onions, sauce and mustard on the other one. A large order of French fries, one cola and one lemon-lime drink."

He paid for the food at the first window and picked it up at the next window. Autumn inhaled the aroma of the food while Nathan pulled into a parking place.

"I always thought Jimmy's hot dogs were the best to be found, and I see that hasn't changed," Autumn said as she took a bite of the succulent sandwich.

Nathan's mouth was full, but he nodded. "I stop here for a snack every time I come this way." He didn't add that he often went out of his way to stop at Jimmy's because this was one of the places he associated with Autumn. He was always aggravated at himself when he stopped for he knew it was best to forget her. Although memories of her were painful, he'd always left Jimmy's feeling as if he'd had a visit with her. Now here she was, special as ever, and he didn't know what to do with her.

"Does your mother still live in Indianapolis?"

"Yes. And her life's a lot better now. She's remarried to a man who's been a good provider. He's set my two brothers up in business, so I don't have to help support them now."

"Do you visit them often?"

"Not much. Farmers can't do a lot of traveling unless they have hired help. I'm trying to do everything by myself, except what little help Tony can give me, so I don't have any free time. The family came to Woodbeck Farm for Christmas last year.''

Autumn finished the hot dog and nibbled on French fries.

"I've spent most of my Christmases alone since I left home," she said, not looking at him.

"Do you ever think about the Christmas Eve we met?" Nathan asked.

"Every year! I'd go to a Christmas Eve service in a church near the campus. The rest of the night, to keep from thinking about being separated from my family, I'd recall every minute of the night Noel was born." She didn't add that she cried herself to sleep every Christmas Eve, the only time in the years she'd been gone that she'd allowed herself the luxury of tears. "I'd remember you, Nathan. I always wondered where you were."

He reached for her hand and drew her closer to him. Autumn wanted to throw herself into his arms and cry out the frustration of the past years, but she stifled her emotions. Being friends was better than nothing, but she did lean against his shoulder.

"After I went to work in the Middle East, I was gone four years before I came back to the States. Lots of the workers would come home for Christmas, but I didn't want to spend the money. I wanted to save all I could. I had a dream, and it took money to achieve it. I'd never expected Uncle Matt to leave me the farm, for he had other nephews and nieces. I thought I had to make it on my own."

"I remember you wanted to be a farmer."

"And not just a farmer, but a farmer like Landon Weaver. Even if he refuses to acknowledge that I exist,

I think he's the best farmer I know, and I admire what he's achieved with his Belgian horses.''

Autumn laid her head on Nathan's shoulder and sniffled. Why did being with Nathan reduce her to tears? Was it thinking about the past or worry about the future?

"Thanks for saying that, Nathan. He built Indian Creek Farm into one of the greatest showplaces in the Midwest. I'd been Daddy's shadow for years, and I loved him more than anyone else. I couldn't stand it when he turned on me. I suppose that's the main reason I left home.''

Although it had hurt Nathan when she'd chosen her father rather than him, he didn't blame her even then. He didn't want this afternoon to be sad for her, so he put his arm around her shoulders and said, "That Christmas Eve was special for me, too, and when I was lonely, thinking about Noel's birth always lifted my spirits.''

Autumn took a tissue from her pocket and blew her nose. She moved away from him a little so she could see his face.

"Have you seen Noel? Doc Wheeler told me that Daddy still owns her and she's had several foals.''

"I'm not welcome at Indian Creek Farm, so I haven't been close to her. Mr. Weaver uses her in his six-horse hitch at competitions, and I've picked her out of the others at the county fair by that little red star on her nose. She's a magnificent animal.''

Autumn's blue eyes sparkled through the tears she'd stifled. "So the star's still there! At first, that was the only way I could tell Noel from the other foals.''

"You sure were excited that day you came home

from college and picked her out of the herd! I guess I never did buy the meal I owe you.''

"But you didn't accept my bet. Besides, you fed me today.''

"Hot dogs don't count. We'll find time for a real dinner before Doc Wheeler gets back and you leave.''

Her heart rejoiced and was saddened at the same time as they drove back to Woodbeck Farm. She was happy to know that he'd dwelt as much on the past as she had and he wanted to continue seeing her. But he apparently had no interest in making any long-term commitment to her.

"Are you coming to the picnic, Saturday?'' he asked as she got in her car to go back to town.

"Probably not,'' she said. "Trina or I will have to keep the clinic open, and it might be better if she brings Dolly.''

"Who is Dolly?'' She wondered if he'd noticed how many common characteristics he and Dolly shared.

"She's Trina's niece, whose mother provided us a home away from home while we were in school. She's been good to us, and we volunteered to take care of Dolly this summer. She's a nice kid.''

"If you can't make it to the picnic, stop by when you're out this way. I'd like to show you the improvements I'm making at the farm and the plans I have for the future.''

"Will do!'' she promised and waved goodbye.

At noon the next day, Autumn stopped at a cafe for a quick lunch on her way out of town. She didn't know any of the workers nor did she recognize the few customers. She took a booth and sipped on the cold water the waitress placed on the table. She fiddled with a wooden puzzle placed on the table to calm customers while she waited for her food.

The waitress brought her salad and sandwich and she ate hungrily. It had been a hard afternoon. She paid no attention to the other patrons of the restaurant until she became conscious of someone standing beside her booth. Her eyes lifted slowly. A tall, slender man with blond hair and smiling, brilliant green eyes, holding the hand of a girl about Dolly's age, looked down at her.

"Hello, Autumn. I heard you'd returned to Greensboro."

At first his identity eluded Autumn, but she finally recognized him as the young doctor her mother thought Autumn should marry.

"How do you do, Dr. Lowe?" she said. "News travels fast around here like it always did," Autumn answered in an indifferent voice. She'd seldom thought of Harrison while she was gone, but when she had, she'd supposed he would have gotten tired of a small place like Greensboro.

"This is my daughter, Christine," Harrison said.

Autumn mustered a smile for the child, who had a sensitive mouth and woebegone eyes, looking as if life hadn't been too kind to her.

"May we join you?" Harrison asked.

"You're welcome to sit here, but I'm almost finished."

"We stopped for milkshakes," Harrison said as Christine scooted across the seat, and he sat opposite Autumn.

"It's nice to see you back in Greensboro," he said. "I needed a summer job and Ray Wheeler wanted an assistant for a few weeks, so it worked out well for both of us," Autumn answered, continuing to eat.

"I understand you're a veterinarian now. That doesn't seem like a profession for Autumn Weaver."

"That's because you didn't know the *real* Autumn Weaver. The plans my mother had for me were not what I wanted," she said, hoping to put to rest any idea he might have that she'd been party to Clara's matchmaking. To divert the conversation from her affairs, she asked, "Are you still practicing here in Greensboro?"

"You haven't heard? My clinic has become a thriving practice. I have several associates and we're working toward establishing a hospital."

"Congratulations!"

Autumn signaled for her bill, and the waitress brought it when she delivered two strawberry milkshakes to Harrison and Christine.

Standing, Autumn said, "It was nice to meet you, Christine."

Harrison stood and took her hand. "I'm pleased to see you again, Autumn. When can we get together for dinner?"

Autumn darted a quick look at Christine, who was sipping slowly on the milkshake, seemingly paying no attention to the adult conversation.

"With your wife's permission, I suppose?"

Harrison laughed. "Apparently you don't know anything about me."

"I'd had no contact with anyone in Greensboro until I met Ray Wheeler a few weeks ago."

Autumn disengaged her hand and started toward the door, but Harrison detained her again. "I've been divorced for two years. Christine lives with her mother in Cleveland, but she's visiting me for a few days. May I telephone you?"

"I don't expect to have any free time. Ray has many customers. Thanks, anyway."

She left the restaurant hurriedly, but she sat in the truck for several minutes before she turned the ignition key. Here was a complication she didn't need! She didn't want the presence of Harrison Lowe to cast a shadow on her relationship with Nathan this time. Surely Harrison wouldn't press his invitation if she didn't encourage him. He seemed to be a fine man, and he would probably be enjoyable company, but he didn't cause her heart to miss a beat. Yet the touch of Nathan's hand sent tremors of anticipation up and down her spine. How important were feelings to a successful marriage? Should one choose a mate by rational thinking rather than by emotional attraction?

As she drove away from the restaurant, Autumn considered what her life might have been now if she'd stayed at Indian Creek Farm to eventually marry Dr. Lowe. If she'd married him, and Christine was her child, would she have gotten over her longing for Nathan? Or when he returned to Greensboro, would she still want him as she did now?

On Wednesday, Autumn had a late-afternoon call to a farm north of Greensboro to assist in a difficult calf birth, and it was after seven before she started home. When she realized she'd be late again, she notified Olive that she'd stop at a restaurant for supper. The day had been hot and muggy, and Autumn turned off the air conditioner and rolled down the windows. The breeze felt good on her face. She liked the sensation of wind blowing through her hair.

She didn't find a place to eat until she came to a truck stop on the outskirts of Greensboro. She drove into the parking lot and stopped beside a red truck, recognizing it as Nathan's. Sacks of feed filled the pickup's bed.

Autumn hesitated before she turned off the truck's engine. Should she drive on and find another place to eat? If she went inside, would Nathan think she was following him? The desire to see him outweighed the possible consequences, so she stepped out of the truck and locked it.

Passing through the glass doors of the restaurant, she saw her windblown appearance and she stopped short. Her natural curls had been stirred by the wind and her hair was fluffed out so much she didn't think a bushel basket could cover it. The heat of the day and the wind off the road had turned her normally rosy complexion only a few shades lighter than her hair. She was a mess! But she lost her chance to retreat when she looked through the window and saw Nathan sitting at a booth. He'd seen her, too, so if she left now, he'd think it was because she didn't want to encounter him. She'd pretend she looked neat and tidy.

She opened the door and strolled to his booth.

"Mind if I join you? I'm running late, so I missed Miss Olive's meal."

He gestured to the seat opposite him. "Sit down. I've just ordered. I went to a meeting of the Angus Breeders Association over in the next county this afternoon, then stopped for feed and other farm supplies. I'm running late, too, and I wasn't in the mood to cook tonight."

The waitress brought the menu, and Autumn ordered. "I'll have broiled chicken, baked potato, glazed

carrots, and garden salad. I'll want coffee with a chocolate chip cookie later on, but now I'd like a pitcher
of water with lots of ice.''

"I didn't suppose you ever ate anything but hot
dogs," Nathan teased after the waitress left their table.

"Only when I'm really hungry."

"Had a hard day?" Nathan asked.

"It's been a hot day and a disappointing one. I was
out on a calf delivery, but the farmer waited too long
to call me. I couldn't save the calf. The cow survived,
but it depresses me when I have a failure. I always
wonder if Ray could have done a better job."

"I'm sure he wouldn't have asked you to take over
for him if he didn't think you could do the work."

"He doesn't know what kind of work I do. I met
him at a veterinarians' conference in March, and that's
the first time I'd seen or talked with him since I left
Greensboro. He took me out to lunch, but we didn't
talk more than a couple of hours. I think he invited
me to work for him on impulse as if he had an ulterior
motive, rather than just the need for someone to look
after his customers while he's away."

"You're qualified for the work, aren't you?"

"You don't graduate from vet school unless you're
qualified, but I haven't had any experience on my
own."

"Didn't you help Doc Wheeler when you were a
girl?"

"Lots of time, and I loved the work, but I still wonder when something goes wrong if I've messed up
some way."

"You impressed me with your skill and knowledge
when you treated my cow. I'm sure you're doing all
right."

His unexpected praise suffused Autumn with a warm glow.

The waitress approached with their salads and Autumn excused herself. "I'll make a quick trip to the rest room. I washed in cold water before I left the farm, but my hands need soap and *hot* water. Don't wait for me."

Nathan almost groaned aloud watching her go down the narrow hallway to the rest room. With her hair blown in every direction, her face flushed with heat and wind, she looked like she did when she was eighteen. Even when he'd thought Autumn was spoiled and was disappointed in her when she wouldn't defend him to her father, her beauty had appealed to him.

He'd believed the times they'd spent together had been nothing but a summer's flirtation to her. Now he wasn't so sure. Why hadn't she married? There must have been other men besides Dr. Lowe who would have been drawn to her physical and inner beauty. Had she thought of him all of these years as he'd thought of her? The more he saw her, the more she fascinated him. How many times could he see her without grabbing her and kissing her the way he'd dreamed of doing for years?

In the rest room, Autumn tried to corral her hair, but without a comb or brush, she couldn't do much, so she bathed her face in cold water, washed her hands and rejoined Nathan. He'd waited for her, and when she sat opposite him, he reached for her hand, bowed his head and said a few words of thanks for their food.

They chatted briefly as they ate, and while waiting for their dessert to be served, Nathan relaxed in the seat and said, "I should be home working. Taking a day off for a meeting is a luxury I can't afford during this busy season."

"We've been busy, too. I don't know how Ray can handle all this work alone. I don't blame Miss Olive for being concerned about him. She's hinted that I'd make a good assistant for him."

"Are you interested?"

"I don't know," she said, hesitating as the waitress brought their dessert. Nathan ate a piece of apple pie with vanilla ice cream, while Autumn nibbled at the cookie she'd ordered.

"Tell me the subject for the lesson next Sunday," she said, "and I'll study in advance. I have a lot to learn about the Bible."

"We'll be continuing our study of Jesus's Sermon on the Mount, where he warned His followers not to store up earthly treasures. It's a lesson I need, for sometimes I get so busy trying to make a success of my farm that I don't take time for Bible study and prayer."

"It was the same way when I was in vet school and working every evening. I found time for everything except my spiritual nourishment."

Nathan seemed in no hurry to leave, and although Autumn knew she should at least make contact with the clinic, she didn't want to interrupt this moment. Their opportunities to meet would be limited, so she didn't want to hurry away. The restaurant was almost empty and she wasn't concerned about occupying the booth for an extended time. He talked about the meeting he'd attended that afternoon, his plans for the farm, and how expensive it was to purchase the equipment he needed.

"My uncle's machinery is mostly old, but I go to

farm sales, and I've accumulated quite a few good pieces of equipment. I'm slowly moving toward my goal of having a thriving farm, but I can't let my desire for that crowd out life's more important aspects.''

''The alienation with my family stands in my way of being the kind of Christian I should be.''

''You haven't seen any of them since you returned?''

She shook her head.

''Your folks will come around. I'd venture to guess that your dad is eager to see you. You're his pride and joy.''

''I used to be, but not any more. I wish I could make up with my family before I leave again. I've driven the truck by the farm several times and wanted to stop to see my parents, but I was afraid of how they'd treat me. I dialed the phone number one day, and the line was busy, so I decided that was God's way of telling me to wait a while. Ray had told me how bad things were with my folks. I believe he persuaded me to come to work for him so I could be reconciled with Mother and Daddy.''

Nathan wondered if that was the only reason. He'd been puzzling for days over Ray's statement when he'd told Nathan he would be gone for a couple of months. ''I've got a bright new helper coming in. It might be good for you to have another vet around for a while.'' Was Doc Wheeler also matchmaking? Ray had never mentioned Autumn's name to him, but he wondered how much the veterinarian knew about the things that had happened between them.

When the waitress brought their bills, Nathan took both of them. ''This one is on me.'' Grinning slightly, he said, ''As I recall, I owe you a meal.'' At her startled gaze, he added, "You *did* recognize Noel when I didn't think you could."

"Oh! I considered that paid when we went to Jimmy's last week."

Reaching for his billfold, he handed the waitress three ten-dollar bills. "That wasn't much of a meal—just a nostalgia journey into the past. I've been wondering if we shouldn't forget the past and start building on the present."

Autumn didn't want to forget some of the things that happened between them, so she found it difficult to respond to that remark.

They walked in silence to the parking lot. Autumn stopped by the cab of the vet truck and Nathan imprisoned her by placing both hands on the truck. He leaned toward her, his eyes warm and tender.

"Don't you have a few pleasant memories of the past?" she whispered. "All I had to sustain me for years were memories. I'd have died if I hadn't focused on the few good moments we had together. Didn't you ever think about seeing me again to resolve the differences we had?"

"Maybe in my dreams. I'll admit I've always been sorry your father knocked me down that day before I finished kissing you the way I wanted to."

"He's not here now," she murmured.

He bent closer until Autumn sensed his warm breath on her face and she lowered her eyelids. If he'd kiss her, perhaps the loneliness around her heart would disappear, but she sensed Nathan's hesitancy as he straightened and looked around.

"No, he isn't here, but lots of others are." He motioned toward several people who watched them from the restaurant windows. He dropped his arms and stepped back. "Good night, Autumn. I enjoyed our meal together."

He waited until she drove out of the parking lot, and he smiled and waved at her. Autumn drove slowly back to the clinic. He obviously didn't want to kiss her, didn't want to recall the past. Had she been too pushy again?

Chapter Eight

The evening meal at the Wheeler house was just finished Thursday evening when Elwood Donahue came to the door. After Trina had persuaded Olive to let her take care of the dishes, Olive had gone visiting.

"Is this a bad time to call?" Elwood asked when Autumn opened the door.

"Not at all, unless we have an emergency call. Come in the kitchen. We were washing and drying dishes to give Miss Olive a break. If you're hungry, there's a piece of blackberry pie left."

"Sounds good," he said. "I haven't stopped long enough to eat today. I went to Columbus this morning where a parishioner was having surgery, and I've been busy since I returned home. I always make follow-up calls when we have church visitors, but I'm a bit tardy visiting you."

"We're glad to see you," Autumn said, leading the way into the kitchen.

Trina brought the pie and poured a glass of milk for the pastor. "Sit down and visit with him, Autumn. I'm almost finished with the dishes. Miss Olive won't have a dishwasher,'' she explained to Elwood, ''for she doesn't think the dishes are clean unless she does them by hand.''

''She makes mighty good pie,'' he said. ''I haven't had any fresh blackberry pie since I left my home in North Carolina and went to seminary.''

''Trina and I shared an apartment while we were in college and vet school, and neither of us had time to cook. We existed on canned soup and sandwiches, except for a rare holiday when we indulged ourselves. It's been great to have some home cooking.''

Trina gave a final swipe to the sink top and joined them at the table with a glass of lemonade in her hand. ''Sometimes I feel as if I've died and gone to heaven when I come down to breakfast and sink my teeth in 'made from scratch' buttermilk biscuits. Miss Olive's spoiling us.''

Elwood pushed aside his empty plate, and Autumn replenished his milk glass.

''How did you like our services last Sunday?'' he asked.

''Your message was encouraging to me,'' Autumn said.

''What about the Bible class? Nathan is one of our finest teachers, although he was hesitant about accepting the position. He's very busy at his farm.''

Trina darted a look toward Autumn. ''It was a good lesson,'' Trina said slowly. ''All of us need to hear what the Bible says about forgiveness.''

''I hope you'll continue worshiping with us.''

''I intend to,'' Trina said, ''as long as we're here.''

Autumn knew that Elwood would have noticed Nathan's reaction to their presence on Sunday. If she and

Nathan spent much time together as she hoped, the pastor might as well know why.

"I'll attend church as much as possible," she said. "Nathan and I knew each other several years ago, and we had some problems. I disturbed him when I came to his class Sunday."

"We have other adult classes if that doesn't work out. Can't you and Nathan resolve your differences?"

"I imagine so, but it may take some time."

Wisely, Elwood let the subject drop. "If I might ask, where are the two of you on your spiritual journey?"

"I'm still a fledgling," Autumn said. "My parents didn't go to church, and I was almost twenty when Trina led me to the Lord. The verse in the book of Hebrews that says, 'you need someone to teach you the elementary truth of God's word all over again. You need milk,' describes me exactly. I had to start out like a baby, and it's been a slow process. I have a long way to go before I reach spiritual maturity."

"Don't we all?" Elwood said. "We never reach spiritual perfection in this world, but we can keep praying and striving to become closer to our Lord."

"I'm trying," Autumn said, "but I'm never satisfied with my growth."

Trina patted her on the shoulder. "She's come a long way, Pastor Elwood."

He shoved his chair back from the table and stood. "If there's anything I can do to help either of you, please let me know. Thank Miss Olive for the pie."

After the pastor prayed and left, Trina asked, "Are you going to the class picnic Saturday?"

"Maybe. It depends on how much work we have to do." Although she was in the habit of confiding in

Trina, Autumn hadn't told her that she'd spent most of Sunday afternoon with Nathan and had eaten with him last night.

"Dolly wants to go because the Simpson children will be there, so I suppose I'll go, too. I want her to have a good time this summer. My culinary skills are lacking, as you know, but I can bake a box cake."

With a laugh, Autumn said, "You won't have to. Just mention that you and Dolly are going to a picnic, and Miss Olive will prepare something for you to take."

"I'm afraid we're taking advantage of that dear woman," Trina suggested.

"Not at all," Autumn assured her. "She's proud of *her* culinary skills and loves to bake."

Saturday morning, Trina was sick with a stomach virus, too weak from vomiting to get out of bed. When Autumn got up, Olive was fluttering around giving her medications. "It's a twenty-four-hour virus," Olive said. "Lots of people are sick now."

"I can't be sick that long," Trina moaned. "I've promised to take Dolly to the picnic. This would have to happen when we've got a full schedule."

"Don't worry about the work," Autumn assured her. "I'll handle the morning office calls and take care of the home visits this afternoon. You'll be better by then."

But when Autumn closed the office at noon, Dolly drooped, sniffing, on the back porch step. Autumn sat beside her.

"What's the matter, kid?" Autumn said, gently tugging her long brown hair.

"Aunt Trina is still sick. I can't go to the picnic."

"Maybe you can hitch a ride with the pastor and his wife."

Dolly shook her head. "I've already asked. Pastor Elwood is making a hospital visit in Chillicothe and might not be back in time for the picnic. Mrs. Donahue isn't going."

Autumn went upstairs and looked in on Trina, who sat on the side of the bed, head in her hands.

"I thought I could make it, Autumn, but every time I sit up, my head whirls."

"I'll drop Dolly off at Woodbeck Farm while I'm making my vet calls, and then go back to pick her up later," Autumn offered.

"That will be okay, if you don't mind. I'll ask Sandy to look out for her. I'll tell Dolly to watch for you and be ready when you drive by to pick her up. I appreciate it." She lifted her head and peered at Autumn. "It might be a good idea for you to attend the picnic anyway."

"And again, it might not be a good idea."

Autumn had a call to vaccinate a couple of 4-H sheep a few miles from Greensboro, so she took care of that right after lunch. It was almost three o'clock when she got back to the Wheeler home. Olive came down the walk carrying a picnic hamper and Dolly pranced at her side.

"Miss Olive fixed cookies and a pot of baked beans," Dolly said. Olive set the basket on the floor of the cab, and Dolly hopped into the seat.

"Mmm, they sure smell good," Autumn said. "I hope she saved some for me."

Olive handed her a bag of coconut macaroons. "Here's something for you to munch on," she said, and added, meeting Autumn's eyes in a piercing gaze, "I think you should go to the picnic."

"Too busy, Miss Olive. Ray isn't paying me to neglect his customers. I'm going forty miles out in the country to a turkey farm. The farmer thinks his flock is taking coccidiosis, and I'm going to administer a round of sulfa drugs."

"Harrumph!" was Olive's only answer, and she turned toward the house as Autumn drove away.

"What's 'cockadosis'?" Dolly stumbled over the big word as Autumn picked up speed.

"It's an intestinal disease caused by a parasite, sort of like what Trina has."

"Poor turkeys!" Dolly said.

"You might save some of your pity for me. I won't have a pleasant afternoon. The farmer has a big flock of turkeys."

Sandy and Debbie were watching for them when Autumn pulled into Nathan's driveway. Autumn handed the picnic basket to Sandy.

"Thanks for looking after her, Sandy. Trina is still very sick. What time should I come after Dolly?"

"Anytime after seven o'clock will be okay," Sandy said. "Wish you could stay."

Waving to Dolly, Autumn released the break on the pickup and drove away, not even looking around to see if Nathan knew she was there.

Nathan stood in front of the barn, directing his guests to a hickory nut grove a quarter of a mile away on the creek bank where tables and chairs had been set up for the picnic. Disappointed, his eyes followed the white vet truck until it was out of sight. Although he'd seen her several times this week, he'd looked forward to seeing Autumn again.

When Dolly and the Simpsons gathered around him, he said to Dolly in an offhand manner, "You came all by yourself, huh?"

"Yes. Aunt Trina is sick and Autumn had to work. She's going to stop for me when she gets finished."

Ignoring the guests around him, Nathan watched Dolly walk toward the creek, suddenly struck by the many physical characteristics he shared with the girl. If Autumn and I had gotten married, we could have a daughter like that, he thought. He shook his head to erase what might have been.

Although he'd resented the Weavers' determination to keep him and Autumn apart, a marriage between them would probably have ended in disaster. They were too young. There were too many differences in their cultural backgrounds. Autumn had never wanted for anything. He'd never had all he wanted or needed. The gulf between them had narrowed considerably when he'd inherited Woodbeck Farm, but were their circumstances similar enough now that he could start dreaming again?

Autumn drove into the barnyard at Woodbeck Farm promptly at seven o'clock, but the place looked deserted. Had the guests already gone home and she'd missed Dolly? There were lots of parked cars so she decided they must still be at the picnic area. Two men she'd seen at Community Chapel came around the corner of the barn, and she stepped out of the truck and approached them.

Replying to her query, one of them said, "Nathan took the guests on a hayride, but they'll be back soon. The wagon was crowded so we stayed behind. We've been down in the pasture looking at Nathan's Belgian horse.''

"Oh, I didn't know he had horses.''

"Just the one, I think.''

She still had some work to do, and Autumn knew she should leave and come back for Dolly later, but she found herself walking toward the field the man had indicated. Grazing a short distance from the fence was a filly, her coat glimmering as brilliant as a sunset. The Belgian lifted her majestic head and looked at Autumn suspiciously.

Keeping her ears open for the sound of the returning tractor, Autumn took a handful of grain from the bucket hanging on the post, climbed up on the board fence, and whistled to the animal. The filly was still skeptical of the stranger, but Autumn cajoled her in the soft tones she'd learned to employ when working with her father's draft horses. Sniffing at Autumn's outstretched arm, the animal picked her way gingerly across the green grass, stretched her neck and nibbled the oats from Autumn's hand. Autumn laid her hand on the filly's shoulder. The animal switched her tail and quivered slightly, but Autumn slipped her arms around the filly's neck and buried her face in the soft mane.

"Oh, you're a beauty!''

Wondering how well the filly was trained, Autumn took hold of the halter, tugged gently and led the animal around the paddock a few times. The past returned like a tidal wave as she recalled her youth on Indian Creek Farm and the days she'd spent with their Belgians before Clara decided Autumn had to become a lady.

Engrossed in the pleasurable interlude, Autumn was

oblivious to the passage of time and what was happening around her. She didn't realize that she was no longer alone until the filly snorted and threw up her head. Nathan leaned on the gate watching her! How long had he been there?

Slowly, she led the filly to the gate, picked up a curry comb and started grooming the animal's flanks.

"I know enough about training horses to know I shouldn't have bothered her without your permission, Nathan, but I couldn't resist." Without looking at him, she added, "I miss the Belgians so much. I've never gotten over having to leave them behind." He opened the gate, entered the paddock and she handed him the curry comb. "I shouldn't have been trespassing."

"It's all right, Autumn," he said quietly.

"How long have you had her?"

"She's about two years old. I bought her a year ago from a farmer in Indiana. She's almost ready to enter competition. I bought an old cart, and I hope I can restore it in time to use it for some shows later on this year."

Forgetting her resolve to go slow with Nathan, Autumn said, "If you're pressed for time, I'd love to help you." She patted the Belgian's sleek rump. "I'm so happy you have the filly, Nathan. I remember your dream to own some Belgians. My grandfather started with one animal, you remember."

One of my dreams, Nathan thought, as she stopped petting the animal and turned away reluctantly.

"I could use some help with the filly, if you have any time, Autumn. And with repairing the cart, too. I know you've had a lot of experience with horses."

"I'll find time to help you," she cried eagerly. "It will be relaxation for me."

"I want to be ready to enter her in competition at the county fair. I try to work with the filly every evening after supper, but I haven't started on the cart. Come anytime you want to."

"Great! I'll be here so much you'll get tired of my company."

"I doubt that," he said meaningfully, and his expression brought a blush to Autumn's cheeks.

"I'll have to go," she said. "I suppose the children are back from the hayride now."

"Yes. Dolly was looking for you and someone told her you were in the pasture. I came to get you."

He closed the gate, and Autumn peered through the bars for a last look at the Belgian. As they returned to the barnyard, she knew the tension between them had lessened considerably. Perhaps their mutual love for draft horses was another tie to bring them together.

God, if only this moment could last forever, Autumn prayed. *The past is gone—nothing matters except that we're together.*

The barnyard was almost empty of vehicles when they rounded the corner of the barn. Pastor Elwood and Dolly sat on the house steps.

"Oh, I'm sorry, I delayed you, Pastor, but thanks for waiting with Dolly."

"It was a pleasure," the pastor said. He rose lazily from the step. "Now I have to go home and study my sermon for tomorrow. Thanks for hosting this picnic, Nathan. Everyone enjoyed it. Sorry I was late getting here."

The pastor drove away and Nathan lifted Olive's picnic basket into the cab of the truck. He helped Dolly negotiate the high step while Autumn slid under the steering wheel.

"Thanks, Mr. Holland," Dolly said. "I had a good time. We don't have farms in Wisconsin."

"I doubt the Wisconsin dairymen would appreciate that remark," Autumn said with a laugh. "You'd better say, there aren't any farms in Milwaukee."

Dolly shrugged her shoulders. "Well, whatever, but I've never been on a farm like this before."

Nathan closed the door beside Dolly and stood looking in the open window. He wanted to tell Autumn how much he'd enjoyed talking to her, but he couldn't find the words.

"Oh, I forgot to ask," she said. "What's the filly's name?"

"It's not as original as the name you chose for yours. I call her Beauty."

"That's a fine name. It fits her."

"That's what came into my mind the first time I saw her."

"I think it's a wonderful name. You're on your way, Nathan. You'll soon have several horses."

Chapter Nine

Usually Dolly's chatter amused Autumn, but tonight as she rattled on about the picnic, Autumn wished for peace and quiet. She needed time to think about the subtle change taking place between her and Nathan. She couldn't settle her mind while Dolly talked a mile a minute. When they arrived at the clinic, Autumn carried the picnic basket into the kitchen and asked Olive about Trina.

"She's a lot better now."

"Any calls?"

"No. The telephone hasn't rung all afternoon."

"I have to leave now, but I won't be gone more than an hour."

Autumn drove out of town, heading east on a gravel road, without any destination in mind. When she came to a path that led to Indian Creek, she pulled to the side of the road and parked the pickup, walked to a secluded part of the creek and stared at the rippling stream flowing by.

She wanted to savor again the meetings she'd had

with Nathan this week. They'd shared a closeness, a completeness different from before. Could it be a new beginning for them? This afternoon, he'd been the Nathan she'd dreamed about for years—kind, compassionate, friendly. If she stayed on as Ray's assistant, could they overcome disagreements of the past and make a new beginning?

God, she prayed, *for some reason, the alienation I've had from Nathan has prevented a close fellowship with You. Truth of the matter, I'm all mixed up in my mind. My yearning for Nathan often conflicts with my commitment to You. Help me to make decisions that will be right for Nathan and me. I believe he wants my companionship. And what about my parents? Am I the one who's been wrong all this time? Am I the one to make restitution? I need Your guidance now more than I've ever needed it. Help! Amen.*

Autumn walked slowly to the truck and drove into Greensboro in the twilight. She wanted to go to Nathan again tonight and talk out her frustrations. Had she read too much into his friendliness the past week? Perhaps he'd been so kind this afternoon because he hosted the picnic, and he was exhibiting his company manners. Her heart was too tender from his kindness to withstand a rejection so she stopped at the clinic and entered the week's work into the computer records. She'd wait a few days before she went out to the farm. She'd learned one thing from past mistakes. Move slowly.

She had an emergency at the clinic the next morning, so she missed his Sunday school class, but she did go for the worship service. Nathan smiled at her across the sanctuary, and her heart skipped a beat. At the close of the service, he came to her side and shook hands with her.

"I missed you in class this morning. Trina said you'd had an emergency. Everything go okay?"

She nodded happily. "The case wasn't too serious. A cat with distemper, which could have waited until tomorrow. But the owners were worried."

Sandy stopped by them. "Trina said that Miss Olive went visiting today, so I invited her and Dolly to the farm for a cookout. Why don't the two of you come, too? Tony's going home with a friend, so, Nathan, you can keep Ralph company in an otherwise all-female gathering."

Nathan looked at Autumn.

"I loafed last Sunday while Trina stayed on call, so it's my turn to work if necessary. I'd like to come, but I'll have to bring the telephone."

"Thanks, Sandy. I'll come, too," Nathan said.

"It won't be anything fancy," Sandy warned them in her breezy manner. "Hot dogs, hamburgers and the fixins'."

"Sounds great," Autumn assured her. "Anything you want us to bring?"

"Just an appetite."

At the Wheeler home, Autumn changed into a pair of green cotton shorts, white knit shirt and a pair of brown sandals. She pulled her hair back from her face and secured it with a wide green band. The thought of sharing a meal with Nathan exhilarated her, and happiness shone from her eyes when she took a last look in the mirror. Trina and Dolly were already in the car waiting for her.

The weather had turned hot and dry, and the shade of the widespread oak tree in the Simpson yard was welcome. Ralph carried several lawn chairs from the porch of the two-story farmhouse. He lit the gas grill and spread hot dogs and hamburgers on it. Autumn and Trina helped Sandy carry out the other food— bread, potato chips, cole slaw, melon balls, condiments for the sandwiches and a large chocolate cake. The aroma of cooking meat tantalized Autumn's appetite, and she remembered that she'd only taken time for a slice of toast and coffee that morning.

But when Nathan walked into the group, dressed in a dark-red shirt and white trousers, deeply tanned from his work in the sun, Autumn's stomach quivered and her taste for food changed to a longing for him. His high-bridged nose and slightly jutting chin kept Nathan from being overly handsome, but Autumn had never seen a more appealing man. Their glances caught and held, her blood stirred and she was mesmerized by the gray eyes filled with patience, touched with laughter, conveying his pleasure at seeing her. Autumn pulled at the collar of her shirt and unbuttoned it.

Sandy's sudden appearance from the house with an ice cream freezer broke the spell.

"Nathan," Sandy said, "you're just in time. Help Ralph make the ice cream while the hamburgers cook."

The electric freezer worked fast and the ice cream was ready in a short time. By that time, Autumn's appetite had returned, and as long as she kept her eyes off Nathan, she ate heartily. She ate both a hot dog and hamburger, but refused Sandy's insistence on second servings.

"I'm waiting for dessert," Autumn said. "I haven't had homemade ice cream for years."

Sandy served the vanilla ice cream in bowls with large slices of cake. Autumn had just finished with dessert when her phone rang.

"Ah! Perfect timing," Ralph said. "You must have your customers trained."

Autumn walked away from them, lifted the antenna and answered the phone.

"Sorry to leave good company," she said, when she finished the conversation, "but a farmer seventy-five miles west of here has a cow calving, and he needs a vet. Trina, if you'll drive me into town, I'll pick up the truck, and you can come back to spend the afternoon."

"I'll take you to the clinic and go with you on the call, if you like," Nathan said. "That way Trina and Dolly won't have to interrupt their visit."

With a brief glance at Trina, and without meeting Nathan's eyes, Autumn said, "I'd appreciate your company. On that kind of call, I might need some help."

Inwardly, Autumn was as excited as a teenager on her first date. He wanted to be with her! Time was healing the wounds of the past.

They made a quick trip to Greensboro where Autumn checked the supplies in the truck to be sure she had everything she would need.

"Are you going to change your clothes?" Nathan asked.

"I don't think I should take time. I keep coveralls and boots in the truck, so I can change to that when we get to the farm. The man sounded desperate."

"Who was it?"

She glanced at the note she'd made. "Stanley Wooten. I don't remember seeing that name on Ray's list of clients.''

''He could have gotten a vet closer than you, but Sunday isn't a good time to find help. Ready?''

''Yes. Do you want to drive?''

''I will, if it'll be any help to you.''

She handed him the keys and stepped into the passenger's side of the truck. Keeping to the speed limit, they didn't lose any time as they drove westward. When they neared their destination, Autumn referred to the directions the farmer had given her. An hour and a half after they'd left Greensboro, they drove into the Wooten barnyard.

A sharp-featured, foxy little man with high color and hard eyes bounded out of the one-story house and across an unkempt yard.

''Mr. Wooten...'' Autumn began.

He must have mistaken Nathan for the veterinarian, for he turned on him, saying, ''Now's a fine time for you to get here. The cow and calf have been dead for an hour.''

''Mr. Wooten, *I'm* the veterinarian. I came as soon as you called me.''

''A woman vet! No wonder you're late—probably had to paint your face and get all dressed up before you came. You're too late, so don't expect any pay for your trip.''

Autumn's face blanched, and his vitriolic attitude rendered her speechless.

''*Just* a minute, Mr. Wooten.'' Nathan came to her defense in a quietly controlled voice, but Autumn sensed how angry he was. ''Dr. Weaver came as soon as you telephoned. She left a picnic and didn't even take time to change her clothes. If your stock died, it's your fault because you waited too late to call. Considering your attitude, I'm not surprised that you couldn't find a vet any closer than Greensboro.'' He took Autumn's hand. "Come on, Autumn. You don't have to take this.''

"I'm sorry about the cow and calf, Mr. Wooten,'' Autumn said over her shoulder as she followed Nathan to the truck. She sat close to him, their shoulders touching as he gunned the engine for departure.

She twisted her hands together, and the knuckles whitened. Nathan didn't say anything until they reached the highway. When he picked up speed, he put his arm around her shoulders.

"Aw, come on, Autumn. Don't let it get you down. He's obviously a sorehead.''

"I don't know how we could have gotten here any sooner without breaking the speed limit. If I'd stayed home instead of going to the cookout, I might have made it.''

"You were on your way in less than a half hour. And the cow was probably dead before we left Greensboro. He ranted at you to give him an excuse not to pay for the call.''

"I wouldn't have charged him anyway. But this incident points out to me that a lot of farmers won't want a woman vet tending their livestock. Maybe my parents were right—I chose the wrong profession.''

"You don't believe that, do you?''

She shook her head.

"Neither do I. And one of these days, your parents are going to agree with us. You fought too long to get where you are, to let a cranky little man cause you to lose confidence. We've got an hour's drive back home.

Don't let's spoil it by thinking about that incident. One of these days, you'll laugh about it.''

"I don't know what Mr. Wooten might have done if you hadn't been along. Thanks for coming with me today and sticking up for me when he got nasty."

"At your service anytime you need me, ma'am." His tone of mock servility amused Autumn, she laughed, and they didn't let the irate farmer spoil their afternoon.

They entered a small town, and Nathan removed his arm from around her shoulders as they drove along the narrow streets.

"There's still eight years of your life that I don't know much about," he said, "and I find myself wondering what happened to you during that time."

She laughed. "You wouldn't find anything exciting about those seven years I spent at the university, going to school year-round, trying to finish my degree as soon as possible. It's almost like one continuous nightmare. I studied, went to class, worked to pay my expenses, existed on fruit, cottage cheese, canned soups and bread. Studied, went to class, worked..."

"Okay. Okay," Nathan said. "I get the general idea."

"Actually, it's a period of my life I'd just as soon forget. I wasn't happy. I made a lot of acquaintants, but Trina and her sister were the only friends I had. I simply existed, but my goal for the future kept me going."

"I understand. I feel the same way about the time I worked in the Middle East. It was boring, hard work, but I was determined to make something of myself, and I thought that took money. You told me that you and Trina had spent almost a year in Europe. You must have had some interesting experiences there.''

"Yes, lots of them. After the Bible Conference ended, we traveled with a small group of Christians, and it was a time of growing for me. Every day we'd pause for prayer and praise. We worshiped on a ferry boat between England and Holland. We stopped for prayer beneath the Eiffel Tower in Paris. We sang and studied the Bible on the banks of the Mediterranean near Marseilles. During the traumatic school years, I had that to look back to and cherish.''

"Did you travel through the Alps?"

"Oh, yes,'' she said. She knew Nathan was asking these questions to prevent her from brooding over Mr. Wooten, and she was thankful that he was with her. What a miserable drive she would have had back to Greensboro, if she'd faced the man alone!

"Although most people believe that Switzerland has the most spectacular scenery, I liked the Austrian mountains best. We spent a month in a little Alpine village in Austria. It was the tourist skiing season, and many people were visiting from English-speaking countries. We worked in a hotel, cleaning rooms, waiting on tables, and we were welcomed because we could speak English. We got large tips from the tourists. Fortunately, it was our most profitable stop, for we needed the money to buy a ticket back home.''

The hum of the motor and the singing tires on the highway contrasted sharply to the quietness of that Alpine setting. In her mind's eye, she could see the ancient, colorful buildings, the beautifully costumed local residents, and the steep slopes behind the village.

"In most of our travels, we conducted our own worship because we couldn't find many churches with English-speaking services. But in that village, there was a visiting Irish priest who held services in a room at the parish church attended by many of the tourists. It was a cosmopolitan atmosphere. We sat beside people from England, Australia, New Zealand, or the United States, and when we knelt at the altar to receive communion with people we didn't know and might never see again, I was sure that's the way God wants us to worship. It was an awesome experience, and it sustained me in the years to come.''

''Sounds like you had a great time.''

''I'd have never achieved what I have without those experiences. I had to come to terms with myself, spiritually and emotionally, before I could continue with my life. When I came home to the States, the past wasn't buried, but I was determined not to let it stand in my way. Times when I wanted to give up, when I didn't think I had any reason to keep on living, I remembered the high points of our trip. I memorized a Bible verse to give me courage, and I've repeated it over and over. 'I can do all things through Christ which strengtheneth me.'''

Nathan took his eyes from the road briefly to look at her, and she saw admiration in his eyes. ''You're a special person. Not many people could have gone through what you have without becoming bitter.''

''Oh, I've had my bitter moments,'' she admitted.

''But you haven't dwelled on them.''

Nathan pulled off into a highway rest stop. ''Let's stop for a while unless you're in a hurry to get home.''

''I left my phone with Trina, so she'll take any calls. I would like to walk.''

Nathan put his arm around her waist and they walked along the short trails, oblivious to the travelers around them. At a vacant shelter Autumn sat on the table with Nathan on the bench in front of her. She ran her hands through his hair and smoothed down errant locks the breeze had ruffled. How grateful she was to be with Nathan! Right now, all she had from him was friendship, and she wanted so much more, but he was a comforting and pleasant companion. She thought he was slowly gaining his trust in her again. She would have to be content with that.

As they started on toward Greensboro, Autumn asked, "And what about you? Did you see anything of the Middle East except the oil fields? You surely didn't work all the time."

"I took one trip to the Holy Land during the Christmas season. I'd always wanted to be in Manger Square on the night we observe the birth of Jesus. It was disappointing to some extent because the city of Bethlehem is so commercialized. I rather resented people making money on such a holy time. But when I went into the large cathedral and was directed to the tiny niche where the stable might have been, I worshiped Christ, as if I'd been one of the shepherds or Wise Men who came to pay homage to Him."

She wanted to ask if he'd thought of the Christmas Eve they'd spent together, but she said instead, "What other part of the trip was important to you?"

"When we crossed the Sea of Galilee in a fishing boat similar to the ones used in the first century. Jesus had spent so much time on or around Galilee, that I felt He must have walked the same paths I did and had sailed across the same water. We stopped in the middle of the lake to worship, and I felt closer to Jesus at that time than I ever had before or since."

"That's an experience I'd like to have someday, but

I won't be traveling much in the near future. I'll have to pay off my school loans and set up a vet practice before I can travel.''

He didn't answer until they'd driven several miles, and his face was thoughtful.

"I'd like you to know, Autumn, that I thought of you and the Christmas Eve we'd spent together when I knelt before that manger. I didn't think I'd ever see you again, but now God has brought us back together. What are we going to do about it?''

Autumn put her arm around his neck and leaned close to him. She kissed her hand and moved it softly along his lips.

"Thanks for telling me. Patience isn't one of my virtues, but I'm trying to turn the development of our relationship over to God. We'll know what to do when the time comes.''

Chapter Ten

After the satisfying afternoon with Nathan, Autumn was in a state of euphoria, but a call Monday morning from her mother brought her down to earth with a thud.

"Well, Autumn," Clara Weaver said, "have you forgotten you have a family?"

Clara's tone pierced Autumn's heart, and she said more sharply than she should have, "Actually, I was of the opinion I didn't have a family. I've understood the Weavers have disowned me and that Daddy said I was never to come back to Indian Creek Farm."

"Landon is gone for a few days. I want you to come and see me."

"Very well. Let me check my schedule." With bleary eyes, Autumn looked at the appointment book. "I have a call in that direction tomorrow morning. I'll stop by then, if that's convenient for you."

"You're not speaking to a stranger. I'm your mother, in case you've forgotten."

"No, Mother, I have a good memory. I remember many things. I'll be there tomorrow."

The minute she hung up the phone, Autumn was sorry she'd delayed the visit for a day. She knew she wouldn't have a moment's peace until she went home.

As soon as they'd finished their evening meal, Autumn changed into white shorts and a striped, knit shirt and headed toward Woodbeck Farm. Nathan had said he could use her help, and if she could be with him, the evening hours would pass more quickly. If she stayed in Greensboro, she'd fret all evening about the visit to her mother.

Nathan was driving the tractor into a machinery shed when she arrived. He waved and she walked to meet him.

"Do you have time to work on the cart tonight?" she asked. "If so, I'm ready to help."

"I've been in the field all day, so I'll have to shower and change clothes. I'm hungry, too. After I've eaten, we can decide what has to be done on the cart. Do you want to walk Beauty until I'm ready?"

"Shouldn't I prepare something for you to eat, while you shower and change?"

"That would be a big help. There's some spaghetti left over from Saturday. You can heat that and make a salad. I always eat a big breakfast, and it lasts me until evening."

Nathan was a good housekeeper, she decided as she searched his neat refrigerator for vegetables. No dirty dishes in the sink, either. After she'd made the salad, she stirred up a pitcher of instant tea and was putting ice in his glass when he came into the kitchen.

His hair, still wet from the shower, was plastered to

his head. He wore a pair of brown shorts and a multi-colored plaid shirt open at the collar. Holding a pair of socks in his hand, he padded barefoot across the kitchen floor toward a pair of tennis shoes beside the lounge chair. He looked so strong and virile that Autumn caught her breath and looked away. He was the answer to any woman's dream, especially a woman who'd been dreaming about him for years.

Perhaps he sensed her discomfiture, for without speaking, he sat in the chair to put on his socks and shoes. She turned her back and busied herself with scooping the spaghetti into a bowl.

"What kind of salad dressing do you want?"

"I'd like a mixture of French and Italian," he said, "but you don't have to wait on me. I'm used to taking care of myself."

"So am I. But it's been nice to have Miss Olive fussing over me the past few weeks. A little coddling won't hurt you."

He sat at the table and waited while she served him.

"Maybe not. I've never had the chance to find out."

Without looking at him, she asked, "I assume you've never been married then."

He lifted his eyebrows when she glanced his way. "I thought modern marriages were partnerships where the husband couldn't expect to be coddled."

"I guess I'm talking about something I don't know about then."

"Apparently so." He laughed and held out his hand to her. "Come, sit with me. Are you going to eat?"

"Miss Olive served supper before I left."

She took the chair beside him, and he held her hand and thanked God for the food and "for Autumn, who's come to help me."

He started eating, and she took a pecan cookie from a sack on the table and nibbled on it.

"To answer your question—no, I've never been married."

His words fill her with joy, and she wanted to ask why he hadn't married, but she stifled her curiosity and changed the subject.

"I'm going home tomorrow," she said. "Mother telephoned today and asked me. Daddy's gone away for a few days."

"Are you excited about it?"

"I'm afraid. I've always heard that one can't go home again. Maybe it's too late to patch up mistakes of the past."

"The Bible teaches that we need to look toward the future. God forgives and forgets our mistakes, so we should also."

"I wanted to tell you I was going, so maybe you can pray for me tomorrow morning. I've always been a little scared of my mother. She expected perfection from her daughters, and we didn't measure up to her expectations."

"Certainly, I'll be praying for you, Autumn. You're in my prayers most of the time."

"Thanks. I hope you don't mind that I've unloaded my troubles on you. When I was a child, I always ran to Daddy with my problems. I couldn't talk to him about my fears of tomorrow, so I came to you."

"My door's always open to you, and I've got broad shoulders." He patted his bulging, muscular shoulders, and Autumn lowered her gaze, wishing he hadn't called attention to the part of his anatomy that would make a good resting place for her head when she was troubled.

After he'd finished eating, he rinsed the dishes and put them in the dishwasher before they left the house.

"I don't mind cooking, but washing dishes is drudgery to me. I spent some of my hard-earned money on a dishwasher," he said.

He had the cart stored in a metal utility building. The vehicle had two large wheels and a narrow seat on a sturdy frame. The metal parts were rusty and the paint was cracked.

"Whew! This is going to take lots of work."

"I know," Nathan said ruefully. "With all of the farm work I have to do, I'd about given up having this ready for the county fair. When you offered to help, I began to hope again."

Autumn eyed the vehicle critically, trying to remember what the carts at Indian Creek Farm had looked like. "The vehicle looks to be in good condition, but I believe it's sat out in the rain. If we strip off the mottled paint, cover the surface with shiny black paint and touch up the decorative parts with chrome paint, it should be all right."

"That's my opinion, too. When shall we start?"

"Right now," Autumn said. "I always carry a pair of coveralls in the car as well as the truck. I'll put them on and we'll get started. Do you have plenty of sandpaper?"

"Yes. And an electric sander, too."

For the next two hours, they worked companionably, chatting about church activities, community affairs and even the national news. Autumn told him about some of her veterinary classes. He commented on the desert climate of the Middle East and the native customs he found interesting.

Autumn remembered the times in the past when

they'd worked together with her filly, Noel. They'd enjoyed this same peaceful, satisfying camaraderie. Perhaps that's the way it should be. But how could she be only friends with Nathan, when every fiber of her body and every instinct of her heart cried out that she wanted more from him than friendship? Having Nathan for a friend was about like handing a starving man an ice cube and expecting him to survive on it. She'd never tried to analyze why she'd been attracted to Nathan when she was a girl, but the past few weeks, she'd started to understand what there was about Nathan that had kept him in her heart during years of absence.

He was a deeply religious man. It wasn't only that he prayed, read the Bible and taught a Sunday school class. God was a part of his life—everything he had was committed to his Lord. When she considered Nathan, she understood the nature of God. He was kind, understanding, compassionate—characteristics that some would consider signs of weakness. In Nathan's case, these attributes had enabled him to throw off the poverty, uncertainty and unhappiness of his childhood to become the confident, strong, optimistic man he was today.

When Autumn's arms started to ache from the pressure she was putting on the wood, she said, "I'd better stop, now. I have a heavy work schedule tomorrow, and you must be tired, too."

Surveying their work, Nathan said, "We've made a lot of progress though. Thanks."

"I'll come as often as I can," Autumn promised. "Even if I'm on call, I'll bring my phone with me, so I can be contacted."

At the car, he gently pulled her toward him in a

brotherly hug. "I'm glad you came back to Greensboro," he murmured. "I've missed you, Autumn."

That wasn't a whole lot of encouragement for the future, but Autumn cherished every word that proved she was important to Nathan.

The road from the highway to the buildings of Indian Creek Farm seemed a mile long, although it was only half that far. Autumn couldn't believe the change in the property. Not only were the fences no longer white, but quite a few of the palings had fallen to the ground. A house shutter hung askew, the flower beds were weedy, and the lawn hadn't been mowed for weeks. The horse barns still looked good, but not in the prime condition they'd once been.

When Autumn stopped the truck and stepped to the ground, she heard a feeble bark from the back porch. If she needed any more evidence of the passage of time, it was her border collie, Spots, tail wagging, limping toward her on stiff legs. She rushed to the dog, dropped to her knees, and wrapped her arms around him. Gray streaks mottled his black hair. Autumn swiped away the tears threatening to overflow.

"Oh, I'm so glad you're still here, Spots. Are you glad to see me?"

The dog barked, licked her face and ambled beside her on arthritic legs as she went toward the house. No one came to greet her, and she wondered if she should knock or just walk in. She knocked.

The door was opened by her sister, Summer, who except for her shorter stature looked enough like Autumn to be her twin.

"Come in. Mother is in her bedroom."

"Aren't you glad to see me?" Autumn whispered.

Summer's eyes filled with tears and she reached her hands to her younger sister. Autumn hugged her closely.

"It's been terrible around here since you've been gone, Autumn. I wish you hadn't run away."

"There's been times when I've wished the same," Autumn admitted. "But I'm stubborn just like Weavers are supposed to be."

Summer stepped away from Autumn and wiped her eyes. "We'd better go to Mother."

"How is she?"

"You'll have to see for yourself."

"How are you, Summer? Do you have a job?"

"Yes. I have a job as a caregiver," Summer replied without bitterness. "When Mother had a stroke, she sent for me. I quit school and came home, and I've been here ever since." A tinge of rancor entered her voice as she added, "Six years of sacrifice she doesn't even appreciate."

"Why didn't they employ a nurse?"

"Mother demanded my services. I really didn't mind delaying my career for a few months. I didn't realize she wouldn't get well and that the situation would stretch on for years."

"I'm sorry," Autumn said.

At least the house was clean, Autumn noted, as she followed Summer to her parents' bedroom. Mrs. Hayes must still be the housekeeper.

Autumn came to a sudden halt on the threshold of the bedroom. Only the piercing blue eyes provided a clue that the emaciated invalid in the wheelchair was her mother. Clara had never been a fleshy woman, but now her pale skin stretched over a rack of bones. Her reddish-brown hair had turned gray. With some guilt,

Autumn thought that her mother's bad health was due in part to emotional problems. Clara's whole life had been wrapped up in Indian Creek Farm and her three daughters. When Spring married and Autumn ran away, the emotional trauma was probably more than Clara could bear. Had her departure brought on the stroke? she wondered, adding another prick to her already overworked conscience.

"Well, Autumn," Clara said, in a demanding voice that hadn't changed.

Autumn moved to her mother's chair, bent over, and kissed the dry cheek. "Hello, Mother. I'm glad to see you. It's good to be home again." She sat down on a stool at Clara's side.

"I'm happy to hear that, but I find it hard to believe," Clara said with asperity. "You've been gone for eight years without a telephone call or a letter to us. You've been in Greensboro over two weeks and haven't called."

"When I left home, I went to Nashville to visit Trina Jackson. You remember Trina, don't you? She's Bert's cousin who came here for Spring's wedding to Bert. While I was there, Trina's mother had a letter from Spring, who was upset because she'd learned that Daddy said I was never to come home again. Because of his ultimatum, Trina's family agreed not to tell any of you where I was. They kept the secret well, it seems."

"Your father doesn't make all the decisions around here."

"Then I would have been welcomed back home?"

"Naturally!" Clara said, then she added, "Under certain conditions, of course."

"Of course," Autumn said bitterly. "I'd have been

welcomed if I was willing to become a slave to your wishes. That's the reason I left in the first place."

"I thought you left with Nathan Holland."

"That isn't true. I wasn't with Nathan. I didn't have any idea where he was until I came back to Greensboro."

"And you came back because he's here? You don't care enough for your family to visit us, but you come back when you learn from Ray Wheeler that Nathan lives in the community now."

Why deny these accusations? Her mother wouldn't believe her anyway.

"Nathan certainly fell into wealth when he inherited Woodbeck Farm," Clara continued, "and the local residents consider him a successful farmer, but he soon found out he's still a farmhand as far as the Weavers are concerned."

Autumn couldn't resist saying, "There's one Weaver who never considered him a farmhand."

"That's no credit to you," Clara said.

Since she hadn't come here to revive the quarrel with her family, Autumn asked, "What happened to Noel? Does Daddy still have her?"

Pride sparkled in Clara's eyes. Her daughters had disappointed her, but she'd retained her pride in the Belgians.

"Noel is a first-class animal. She's had four foals, and Landon always uses her in exhibitions. As a yearling, she won Grand Champion at a fair in Indiana."

All triumphs she'd missed because she hadn't been an obedient daughter.

"Where did you get the money to finish your education?" Clara demanded, and Autumn supposed it was natural for a mother to want details of a wayward child's life.

"I applied for lots of student loans and worked like a dog." She explained about the cleaning service she and Trina had started.

"My daughter—a cleaning woman!"

"It was work or starve. You and Daddy have always worked. As long as the work is honest, there aren't any inferior jobs. I'd wanted to be a vet for years, and I was willing to make any sacrifice to achieve that goal. It will take a long time to pay off my loans, but I'll make it."

"We wanted to provide a college education for each of our daughters. Spring quit school to get married, and you run off and work at common labor to pay your way through school."

"What about me?" Summer said. "I was willing to accept your support to get an education, but you wanted me to stay at home."

Clara ignored Summer's remark. Almost near the breaking point, Autumn patted Clara's hand and prepared to leave. The longer she stayed, the more she realized what a sad place her home had become. She couldn't hold her tears much longer, and Clara had never permitted her daughters to cry.

"I have an appointment on a farm east of Greensboro in a short time, so I'll have to leave now. I'm going to the barns before I go. I want to see the horses."

"Yes, I remember you preferred the barns to the house," Clara said.

The housekeeper waited for her on the back porch.

"It's high time you came home, Autumn," Mrs. Hayes said. The housekeeper was a heavily muscled woman, and her eyes glittered with stubborn vitality. Mrs. Hayes had never allowed Clara to dominate her.

Ignoring the woman's accusing tone, Autumn said, "Things are worse than I thought they'd be, Mrs. Hayes. Will Mother ever be any better?"

"The doctors say she could have recovered, but when she had the stroke, she didn't want anyone to see her feeble condition. She refused to have a therapist come here, and she wouldn't go to the hospital. She's made a slave of Summer. The girl has to sleep in the small dressing room next to your mother's room, so she's on call day and night."

"Things have come to a sorry pass, it seems."

"Maybe it's time for you to make a difference."

"Perhaps it is, but I have to be accepted first."

Spots followed Autumn to the barn, and the past flooded back as she walked through the open door. The sweet smell of molasses and oats, the tangy scent of hay, and the earthy smell of the mares peering at her from their box stalls hadn't changed. The rest of the farm may have been neglected, but Landon's Belgians were still cared for. Would she know which horse was Noel? Autumn wondered as she walked down the center of the barn fondly observing the chestnut-hued mares.

She recalled the days when she'd dogged Landon's steps. When she'd been happy to be with her father. When he'd encouraged her to learn how to care for the Belgians. She remembered the first time she'd seen Nathan, and the night they'd spent in this building when Noel was born.

Autumn came to the last stall before she found her mare, which she recognized as she'd done years ago by the red star on her forehead. She approached the horse slowly, but almost as if she remembered the time Autumn had helped to give her birth, the mare whinnied and stretched her neck. When she stepped inside the stall and put her hands on the large Belgian, she could no longer hold the tears. She cried, not only for her complicated life now, but for the lost years of her youth and the months she'd missed being with her loved ones. Lost experiences, she could never retrieve.

"Ah, Noel," she whispered, "what would I do if I could live my life over again? Being myself, I don't suppose I'd react any differently, but it's been hard. Hard!"

Chapter Eleven

Autumn couldn't generate any interest in her work for several days after the depressing visit to her home. If it hadn't been for the hours she spent at Woodbeck Farm helping Nathan a night or two each week, she would have had a miserable time.

His encouragement helped her to throw off her despair until a few days later when she encountered her father. On her way to assist a farmer with a calf delivery, Autumn stopped at the post office to pick up a package of vaccine that had been shipped by registered mail.

She parked in front of the one-story brick building, and when she got out of the truck, her father was coming down the walk.

The sight of Landon's beloved face caused Autumn to forget the dissension between them, and she ran toward him with outstretched arms. "Oh, Daddy," she cried, but avoiding eye contact, Landon brushed by her without saying a word.

"Oh, Daddy," she whispered again past the knot in her throat. She turned to watch him as he turned down the street, noting his stooped shoulders and uncertain steps. The package forgotten, Autumn rushed back to the truck, blinded by tears.

So much for coming to work as Ray Wheeler's assistant! How could she live in a town where her own father wouldn't speak to her? Had her actions really been bad enough to warrant her father's rejection? If she thought Trina could handle the vet work until Ray returned, she'd leave Greensboro and *never* return. But could she spend the rest of her life running away? Besides, she didn't want to leave Greensboro until she and Nathan came to terms on their relationship.

After Autumn finished her calls and arrived back at the animal clinic, she learned that Miss Olive was gone for the evening, and Trina had promised Dolly a visit to her favorite pizza shop. Autumn telephoned Nathan.

Still smarting over her father's rejection earlier in the day, she wanted to be with Nathan. She was disappointed when she got his answering machine, although she knew he often worked until almost dark. She left a message, hoping he would find it before he prepared his evening meal.

"Hi, Nathan. I'm coming out to work on the cart tonight. Don't bother preparing supper. It's my turn to provide the food. I'll come about seven o'clock."

After she showered, Autumn looked through the closet in her bedroom, observing her wardrobe with distaste. How long had it been since she'd had any new clothes except the dress she'd bought to wear to her graduation from veterinary school? She had a couple of skirts and blouses that she wore to church. Except for that, her wardrobe consisted of jeans and shirts, most of which she'd bought at yard sales. Short sleeves for summer. Long-sleeved sweatshirts in the winter. She *must* go shopping.

But she didn't have time to shop tonight. She selected a pair of denim shorts and a pink T-shirt, embroidered along the neckline in white yarn. She smiled when she remembered how her mother had always quarreled when Autumn had insisted on wearing pink.

"Never wear pink with a head of hair like yours," she'd said, preferring that her daughters wore pastel shades of blues and greens. When Autumn had gotten old enough to pick her own clothes, she'd sometimes choose pink garments, much to her mother's dismay. They'd been a close family when they were children. Too bad we had to grow up, Autumn thought.

As Autumn finished dressing, she remembered that none of the plans her parents had for their daughters had been realized.

"They couldn't understand," Autumn muttered, "that we weren't robots to move how and where they wanted us to. I figure in their youth, Mother and Daddy were as wilful as their daughters. We had to inherit our traits from somebody."

Autumn brushed her hair back from her face and secured it with a wide band. She strapped on a pair of sandals, happy to get out of the heavy boots she wore all day long. A glance in the mirror showed her eyes glowing with anticipation and a flush on her cheeks.

Trina and Dolly had walked to the restaurant, so she left Ray's truck in the garage and drove her own car. The vehicle was ten years old, but she was thankful it ran as well as it did. Needing to pay off her school debts, she knew it would be a long time before she could afford anything better.

Stopping at a deli in the shopping center, Autumn ordered cheese and turkey subs with all the trimmings, cole slaw, baked beans, apples, cheesecake, and a container of tea with lots of ice. Today's heat had about parched her throat, and she was thirsty.

When she arrived at Woodbeck Farm, there was no sign of Nathan. His truck was parked in front of the house, so he probably hadn't come out of the fields for the night. She went to the paddock behind the barn and tried to make friends with Beauty, but the filly lifted her proud head, ignored Autumn and continued to graze on the far side of the field.

She heard the steady hum of a tractor on the other side of the creek. If Nathan intended to work until dark, the food would spoil. She went to her car and took the deli bags and headed in his direction. A narrow foot bridge provided passage to the other side of the creek and she saw Nathan's tractor coming toward her. He was baling hay, and she inhaled deeply of the pungent aroma of new-mowed alfalfa.

She set the bag of food on the ground, waited in the shade until he was near where she stood. When the baler dropped one huge round bale of hay behind it, she stepped out of the shadows cast by the lowering sun disappearing behind silver-lined thunderheads in the west. Nathan didn't see her at first, but when he did, startled, he braked and stopped. Jumping from the tractor, he ran toward her and grabbed her in his arms.

Momentarily, she sensed that he smelled of sweat and diesel fuel, but what did it matter? She lifted her arms and flicked back the brim of his straw hat so she could have a full view of his face. His gray eyes glowed with pleasure. He was happy to see her! He'd made the first move, so she hooked her arms around his neck and snuggled into his embrace. Happiness burst from her in a quiet, quavery laugh. Her blue eyes offered an invitation.

Nathan lifted one hand and pulled the band from her hair and loosened her hair by threading the curly tresses with his fingers. He drew her face closer to his. With the first touch of his lips, Autumn's eyes closed and as his kiss intensified, she experienced a symphony of sensations. Exultation. Joy. Pain. Sorrow. Peace. Happiness.

When she thought her heart would burst with emotion, Autumn broke the caress and leaned her head on Nathan's muscular shoulder, sensing the dampness of his sweat-soaked shirt on her face. His arms tightened until she could barely breathe as his lips slid down the side of her face to her throat, nibbling her ear on the way by. They'd bridged eight long years in a few blissful moments.

Half laughing, half crying, Autumn murmured, "Oh, Nathan!"

"I've been thinking about you all day. When I looked up and saw you standing there, I couldn't believe you were real. I had to get you in my arms to be sure you weren't a mirage."

"I'd left a message on your answering machine that I'd come out this evening and bring food. When I got to your house, I heard the tractor running, so I headed this way. Perhaps I shouldn't have interrupted your work."

Nathan had intended to work late tonight to finish baling the hay before it rained. Without a glance at the lowering clouds to the west, he released Autumn, went to the tractor and turned off the engine.

"Forget the work! I'm hungry for food and *you.* Let's eat." He knew later on he'd have second thoughts about letting a field of hay get wet and tell himself he was still too poor a man to pursue a relationship with Autumn. But he saved those warnings for the long night hours when he lay awake with his memories of Autumn, knowing he had to be content with those. Savoring her response to his kisses, did he dare hope there was a future for them?

Autumn picked up the bag of food. "Why don't we eat here? Then you can go back to work, and I'll go home." She picked up a handful of alfalfa and sniffed. "This hay is too good to risk getting it wet. I thought we could work on the cart tonight, but this hay is more important."

"Not many women would be aware of that. But you're Landon Weaver's daughter and you'd have learned a lot from him."

He took a cushion off the tractor's seat and dropped it on the ground for Autumn. As she spread out the food, he thought what a great wife she'd make for a farmer. But he couldn't think that far yet. It would be years before he'd be out of debt.

She handed him a cup of iced tea, and he drank it greedily. He lounged on one elbow and noticed how neat she looked compared to his dirty, sweat-stained clothes. There was a dark smudge on her pink T-shirt, and he was sure it hadn't been there before he'd hugged her.

Grinning tenderly at her, he said, "Sorry I got your T-shirt dirty. Should I apologize for grabbing you so unceremoniously, dirt and all?"

"No apology needed sir," she replied with a grin.

He straightened when she placed his food on a napkin and handed it to him.

"Say! This food is good," he said, making short work of the sub.

"The best Martin's Deli has to offer."

"What kind of cook are you?" he asked with a grin.

"I have no idea. I've never had a chance to find out. Mrs. Hayes and Mother did all the cooking at home. Miss Olive waits on us hand and foot. And when I was in vet school, it was cheaper and faster to eat in the cafeteria. I did learn a lot about opening soup cans though."

He finished the rest of his food and stretched out on the ground, hands behind his head. Autumn packed all the utensils and papers into the bag and sat close to him. She patted her legs. "Want a more comfortable pillow?" she invited.

He rolled closer to her and rested his head on her knees. She pushed his damp hair back from his face and brushed soft fingers across the roughness of his beard.

"I haven't shaved for a couple of days," he said, "as you can probably tell. I've been working day and night to get this hay baled. I rented the baler, and I want to return it as soon as possible."

"Then I should leave and let you get back to work."

"Not just yet. I'll rest a while. I only have another

hour's work, and according to the weather report, the storm won't arrive until late tonight."

She wiped his sweaty face with a napkin.

"I saw Daddy this morning."

"And?"

"I spoke to him and he walked by as if he hadn't seen me." Her lips trembled. "If heartache was fatal, I think I'd have died right then. I suppose I've always held out hope that he wasn't really mad at me. I don't doubt it now."

Nathan's lips tightened, and he took her hand and kissed her fingers. "He has no right to treat you that way."

"I suppose he thinks he does. But it hurt. I was almost sorry I'd come home and I wanted to leave."

Nathan's grip tightened. "But you won't?"

"No. I've stopped running away. I'll stay until Ray gets home as I promised. After that, I can't tell."

"I don't want you to leave, but that's all I can say now."

Autumn leaned over and kissed his forehead. "I don't want to leave either, but I don't know how I'll feel when I have to make that decision. Right now, I'm going back to Greensboro so you can go to work."

He unlimbered his sturdy frame, stood and stretched.

"Thanks for breaking the monotony of this long day, Autumn. I've been working here since daylight, and I hadn't eaten any lunch."

"Is there anything I can do at the barn before I leave?"

"Well, since you asked, you might check to see if Beauty has enough grain, and put some hay down for the two cattle I have in the barn. They've been sick, and I want to be sure they don't have anything contagious.''

"Consider it done.''

Nathan pulled her into his arms again, and he marveled at how well she fit into his embrace. Could Autumn Weaver be his for the asking? Did he dare hope again?

Chapter Twelve

Saturday morning, the clinic phone rang and Trina answered.

"Just a minute," she said, and rolling her eyes with a hand on her heart, she handed the phone to Autumn.

From Trina's actions, Autumn figured the caller was Nathan, and she smiled as she answered.

"I'm going to an auction this afternoon," Nathan said. "Want to go along?"

"Sure do. What time?"

"The auction doesn't start until two o'clock, but I want to be early. There's a hay baler for sale, and I want to look it over before I bid on it. What time can you leave?"

"We close the clinic at noon." Trina was making frantic, waving gestures at her, which Autumn took to mean, she was to go sooner than that. "But I can leave early. You set the hour."

"It's a thirty-minute drive, so if we leave a little before noon, I'd have plenty of time. We can eat at the auction."

"I'll be ready. Thanks, Nathan."

When Autumn replaced the phone, Trina lifted her clenched fist in a victory salute. "Yes! Where are you going?"

"To a farm auction."

"A farm auction!" Trina groaned. "That's not very romantic."

Autumn laughed from sheer joy. "I doubt if Nathan is in a romantic mood. He's going to buy a hay baler and that is a big decision for him. He's short of money, and the baler may cost more than he can afford."

Trina gave a sigh of resignation. "At least he's invited you to go someplace. Maybe that will be the start of something."

"*Something* has already started. We only have to decide how it's going to end."

"An auction!" Trina muttered, shaking her head. "At least, go and dress in something romantic. I can take care of things here."

"I'll shower and change clothes, but I won't look any different than I do now. People wear jeans and shirts to auctions. We're in farm country, Trina."

After she washed and dried her hair, Autumn started to brush it away from her face and neck to the top of her head, but she paused with the brush in her hand. She shook her hair free. Nathan had never said, but she knew he liked her hair loose around her shoulders. As thick as her hair was, she was uncomfortable on hot days, but she could stand a little discomfort to make Nathan's eyes light up.

Which they did when he stopped before the Wheeler home. Autumn came down the walk to meet him, wearing a blue shirt and lightweight denims. He opened the door for her.

"Don't ever cut your hair, Autumn. I like it that way."

She laughed at him and lightly pinched his arm through his denim shirt as he pulled away from the curb.

"If I didn't cut my hair, I'd be sitting on it in a few years." She pushed back his wide-brimmed hat. "What if I asked you not to cut your hair?"

"That's different," he insisted. "I like your hair that way."

"I know you do, and so do I, but it has to be trimmed occasionally, or I'd look like a red tumbleweed. I wore it down to my shoulders today because I wanted to please you. Isn't that enough to satisfy you?"

"Yeah," he assured her with a lazy smirk. "So that will be the least of my worries today."

"What's worrying you?"

He handed her a sale bill. "I don't know how much I can afford to pay for that baler if I buy it. Read the description and tell me what you think."

"If you brought me along to advise you on this piece of equipment, you wasted your time. Horses, I know. I don't have any knowledge of machinery."

"That wasn't the reason I invited you."

"Do I dare ask why?"

"I hadn't seen you for a couple of days."

"I guess that's reason enough. What else are you going to buy besides the baler?"

"Nothing. And I may not buy it. My uncle had lots of machinery, and although most of the pieces are old, I'm getting along with them. But I need to upgrade when I can."

They followed the sale signs and came to a wide

field, filled with automobiles and trucks, and with various pieces of farm machinery grouped next to a large barn.

"Is this just a machinery sale?" Autumn asked.

"No. Turn the sale bill over. There's quite a lot to buy."

"I see there are antiques and old glassware. I might buy something for Miss Olive. She's been very good to us this summer, and I'd like to buy a gift for her."

"Then I'll get a card for you so we can keep our bidding separate."

After they registered and got two numbered cards for bidding purposes, Nathan stopped by a food stand. "The selling will be at the house, but I'll look at the hay baler and see what I think." He handed her some money. "Will you buy some food for us while I check out the machinery?"

"What do you want?"

"Whatever you buy, I'll like." He arched his eyebrows at her. "You know my tastes pretty well."

Was he talking about more than food?

She bought hot dogs, wedges of apple pie and large cups of iced tea and waited for him when he returned.

"What do you think of the baler?" she asked as they waded through the trampled grass toward the two-story house.

"It's in good shape. I'd like to buy it if the price isn't too high."

They sat on the grass to eat their lunch, then walked among the tables holding items for sale. Books, dishes, bedding, household equipment and boxes of junk.

"It's an estate sale," Nathan explained, "and everything goes. We're going to be here a long time. Are you in a hurry?"

"Not at all. Stay as long as you like."

Six hours later, they started home hauling a hay rake behind the truck. Nathan had bid on the hay baler, but when the bids reached ten thousand dollars, he'd had to stop bidding. He also bid on a tractor, but it had sold for more than the hay baler. He'd successfully bid on the hay rake for twenty-eight hundred dollars, but he thought he'd gotten a bargain. As they rattled and bumped over the unpaved road pulling the hay rake behind them, Autumn said, "I'm sorry you didn't get the baler."

"Don't be. I've been getting along renting a baler. It would be more convenient to own one, but I don't have that kind of money. Actually, Autumn, I'm land poor. I own a good farm, but my operating money is limited and it will be for many years. I don't want to go in debt for machinery if I don't have to. I had the money to buy the rake, so I'll be content with it."

Autumn had bought an antique wooden butter mold for Miss Olive, and a porcelain figure of a Belgian horse for Nathan.

"This horse is a present for you. The only part of your house I've seen is the kitchen and bathroom, but you don't have one decorative item."

"You know the reason I don't have knickknacks?"

"I can't imagine."

"I don't want to dust them."

"You won't have to dust this one either. I'll stop by at least once a week to dust it."

"Yes, but who's going to do it if you leave Greensboro?"

"That will be your problem," she said. "And speaking of purchases, you bought two items—very incongruous items, I might add. A hay rake and an empty picture frame.''

''I don't think they're incongruous for I need both of them. I have hay to rake and a picture to frame.''

''What kind of a picture?''

''I'll show you when I get it framed.''

''Do you enjoy sparring with me, Nathan?''

His gray eyes flicked over her face and his lips broadened into a wide smile. ''It *can* be entertaining, but I just like to be with you, Autumn, no matter what we're doing.''

''Thanks for asking me to go today. It's been fun.''

Because Nathan needed to get home and take care of his animals, they didn't stop to eat, but it was already dark when they pulled into the driveway at the clinic. The past ten miles Autumn had sat close to him, her left hand gently massaging his neck.

After giving her a brief, tender kiss, Nathan drove on home, already scheming of some way to see her again soon.

Two days later, Summer telephoned, and in an amused voice, she said, ''Daddy is away for a couple of days and Mother wants you to come for dinner tomorrow night. She said to bring your co-worker and *that* child with you.''

A royal command, Autumn thought wryly, but she did want Trina to see the farm, and their sojourn in Greensboro was getting shorter all the time.

''All right, we'll come by six o'clock if we don't have any emergencies. If so, I'll telephone.''

Autumn turned to Trina with a half smile on her face. ''We have a dinner invitation, and I suppose I

should have cleared it with you before I accepted."
She repeated what Summer had said.

Trina laughed. "Of course, we'll accept! I thought
Indian Creek Farm was the most beautiful place I'd
ever seen when we came for Bert's wedding. I'd love
to see it again. I can still see you three girls approaching the gazebo on the lawn."

Dreamily Autumn thought of that tranquil day ten
years ago when the farm was arrayed in all its glory,
and when she was in the good graces of her parents.
Even if Clara hadn't approved Spring's marriage to
Bert, she'd arranged a beautiful wedding for them.

The wedding procession had been unique. With regal dignity, two Belgian horses, decked out in black
harness embellished with silver, pulled a shining black
barouche. The horses, magnificent heads held high,
tails braided and white manes flowing over their necks,
masterfully lifted their large hooves and moved forward in step to a lively rendition of "Trumpet Vol-
untary," played with gusto by the five-man band.

Tux-clad Landon Weaver, perched on the high front
seat, held the reins of his prize-winning mares. Clara
sat beside Spring, a vision of loveliness in snowy
white wedding garments. Summer and Autumn were
seated on the opposite side, garmented in simple, pastel dresses. Landon had often glanced over his shoulder, and it was difficult to determine the object of his
greatest pride. Was it the matched Belgian horses or
his three beautiful daughters?

Recalling that day, Autumn wondered how her father could have changed so much?

"I suppose Mother has heard that Dolly looks like
Nathan, and she wants to check it out. Wouldn't you
think she would have more faith in her daughter than

to suspect me of having an affair? I was only eighteen!''

"Autumn," Trina said sternly, and Autumn grinned. When Trina used that tone of voice, Autumn expected a lecture. "Clara Weaver has a strong dominating personality and she structured her whole life around her family. She had a blueprint of how she expected her daughters to turn out, and all of you disappointed her."

Laughter gleamed in Autumn's blue eyes. "Put that way, it does seem as if Mother had cause for a grievance. I guess we were rebellious, thankless daughters."

"I'm not trying to be funny, but you should understand your mother's viewpoint and have a little sympathy for her. Her plans were crumbling, and she thought all of her sacrifices for you had been wasted."

"And my defection was the last straw, even for Daddy," Autumn commented grimly. "It was no secret that I was his favorite daughter, mostly because I spent so much time with him taking care of the horses. Although I'd heard he'd disowned me, I couldn't believe it until he refused to speak to me Monday."

"Many times it's the child you love the most who gives the most pain," Trina said in a solemn voice, as if she spoke from years of experience and wisdom. "You must have caused him a lot of grief when you left, and no doubt your mother blamed him for your leaving because he'd allowed you to spend so much time with the Belgians."

"I'm sorry for many of my actions of the past, but I've never regretted that I defied her about dating Harrison. Mother had no right to dominate our lives, and she's still doing it. She won't let Summer leave her side, and I have no doubt she'd like to interfere in my decisions now.''

"You're never going to change her. God can change her will, but you can't. We need to pray for a softening of your mother's heart.''

"I do pray for her and for my attitude toward her, but I won't have her meddling in my life. She still won't accept Nathan, and since Harrison is divorced, she might take it into her head to start matchmaking again. Mother would love to have one of her daughters marry a doctor.''

Trina shrugged her slender shoulders. "Well, what mother wouldn't? Accept your mother as she is and learn to live with her.''

The bell over the door jingled, indicating their first customer had arrived, and Autumn stood up and put on a smock. They faced a full morning in the surgery room.

"Wait until after we've been to dinner tomorrow night before you give me a lot of advice. You don't know Mother as well as I do.''

They arrived at the farm a half hour before the dinner hour to allow time for Dolly to see the Belgians. The mares had already been turned into the pasture, so while Trina and Dolly stayed behind the gate, Autumn walked to the nearest Belgian and led her over to the fence. She recognized the mare as Tulip, Noel's mother. The mare nuzzled Autumn's head and shoulders. As Autumn leaned against the huge horse, she was overcome with a dreadful sense of loss. She'd lost eight years of her life estranged from her family. If she had it to do over again, would she have obeyed her parents and stayed in Greensboro so she could be near her father and the farm she loved so much? Was Nathan worth the sacrifice she'd made for him?

Ignoring the tears threatening to overflow, Autumn coaxed the Belgian to the fence where Dolly climbed up on the palings and petted Tulip's side. Trina took Autumn's hand and squeezed it, a compassionate look in her eyes.

"Are you all right?" she whispered.

"Yes, but whenever I come home, I'm reminded of the happiness of my first eighteen years and how miserable I've been since then. I'm almost sorry I came back to Greensboro. I'd pushed the past into the background, learned to live with the pain. I was making a new life for myself. I don't know whether I'm wallowing in self-pity or what, but I can't find peace of mind anywhere."

Trina laid her hand on Autumn's shoulder. "It's going to work out all right. God is in control of the situation, and I'm praying He will give you the grace to accept whatever happens. He had a purpose in bringing us to Greensboro."

Tulip wandered away, and Dolly said, "And this is where you lived when you were a little girl?"

Autumn nodded. "I perched on this fence and petted Belgian mares before I could read and write. Daddy didn't have any sons, but he often bragged that I was as good with horses as any boy could be. He encouraged me to learn everything I could about the equine industry. I could have lived the rest of my life on this farm, but then Mother decided I should be a debutante. And speaking of Mother, we must go to the house. It's inexcusable to be late for a meal here."

The evening sun cast mellowing rays over the white ancestral house camouflaging the ravages time had brought to the home. Shades of yellow accented the scalloped shingles on the house. The stained glass in the transom above the door and in the two windows along the front shone like dewdrops gleaming on a verdant, green pasture. With its original slate roof, large verandas, conical tower, two bay windows, and a second-floor balcony, the house looked much as it had when it was built a century ago.

Ray had left instructions with Olive that Autumn and Trina should be paid every two weeks, so having some cash in their pockets, they'd bought a bouquet of carnations for Clara. They stopped by the car to get the flowers, which Dolly proudly carried into the house. Autumn watched her with amusement, thinking how nice it would be to have a daughter like Dolly, especially one who looked so much like Nathan. Everywhere she turned, there was something to remind her of Nathan. No wonder he dominated her thoughts.

Clara sat in the living room, dressed in a black silk dress with silver heirloom jewelry around her neck and in her earlobes. Summer stood by her chair.

"Hello, Mother," Autumn said, still disbelieving that this shriveled woman could be the matron who'd ruled like a queen over Indian Creek Farm. Had she been the cause of Clara's downfall, Autumn wondered?

"You remember Trina, don't you? And this is Dolly, Trina's niece."

Dolly stepped forward proudly. "Here's some flowers for you, Mrs. Weaver. I helped choose them, but Aunt Trina and Autumn paid for them." Looking at Summer, who stood beside Clara's chair, Dolly continued, "You look like Autumn—you must be her sister. You're pretty, too."

Summer smiled slightly. "So I've been told. Would you like to see some pictures of us when we were about your age?"

"Yes. There's nobody but me in my family. It must be fun to have sisters."

"That's debatable," Summer said, with a teasing glance at Autumn. She took Dolly's hand. "We have enough pictures of the Weaver sisters to fill a gallery, but let's look in Daddy's office first. The best ones are in there."

Clara said to Trina, "Now tell me what you hear from Spring and Bert." With a stern look at Autumn, she added, "Unfortunately, my daughters aren't letter writers, so I seldom hear from Spring."

We learned that from you, Mother, Autumn thought, remembering the days she was away at college, homesick for news of the family. She'd always looked forward to a message from her mother, only to open an envelope with a few terse words confined to the health of the family and details of household management.

Trina pulled a chair close to Clara. "My aunt, Bert's mother, went to visit Spring and Bert a few months ago, so I can give you some firsthand information. They're getting along fine, and their two children are adorable. Their term in Bolivia will be up in a few months, and they'll be coming home on furlough. There's a possibility they may stay in the States."

Clara was engrossed in Trina's news, so Autumn joined Summer and Dolly in the office. A large oil portrait of the three daughters, painted when Autumn was ten years old, hung on the wall opposite Landon's desk. The rest of the wall held framed photographs of Autumn and her sisters, many of them taken with the Belgian horses. One of the pictures showed Spring in her wedding dress flanked by Autumn and Summer in their bridesmaids' finery standing in front of a white gazebo. The large picture of Autumn seated on a black, silver-ornamented cart, holding the reins of a draft horse, which Landon always said was his favorite, had been taken on her fourteenth birthday.

Summer settled Dolly behind Landon's desk and handed her a photo album. While the child slowly turned the leaves of the album, Autumn said quietly, "I'm surprised my pictures are still displayed. I figured they'd remove all trace of me from the house."

"Although neither of them would admit it, they've missed you too much for that. Mother and Daddy haven't been happy together since you left. Each blames the other for your departure."

Summer turned a frame on the desk holding Autumn's high school graduation picture, and Autumn sighed at the photo. On that day she thought the whole world lay at her feet.

Without bitterness, Summer said, "You always were Daddy's favorite. Time and anger can't change that."

"I find that hard to believe when he passed me on the street this week and didn't even acknowledge my presence."

"You stick around a while and he'll get over it. I've seen him sitting at this desk too often with your photograph in his hands to believe he's never going to forgive you."

Autumn laid her arm across her sister's shoulder.

"Why don't you leave and get on with your life, Summer? Surely they can afford a nurse to care for Mother?"

Summer reached for Autumn's hand. "Money can't

buy family, and Mother has been so afraid. She'd have died if I hadn't stayed here."

Autumn lowered her voice. "I can't believe Mother is afraid of anything."

"She's afraid of growing old and dying without her daughters, and I want to help her. I'm resigned to staying here now. For the first year, I felt like a prisoner and I was rebellious, but I've come to terms with my situation."

"Don't you have any time to yourself?"

"Very little."

"I wish I could relieve you, but even if I came to work at Ray's clinic full-time, I couldn't help with Mother when Daddy forbids me to come home. I'll feel guilty when I leave you with all this responsibility after Ray gets back, but I can't stay here under the circumstances."

Summer cast an oblique glance toward her younger sister. "Not even to be near Nathan Holland?"

Autumn flushed. "I'll admit I didn't forget Nathan, and I was happy to see him when I came home. But I don't know what the future holds for us."

"Mother hasn't said, but the more she hears about Nathan's rise to a place of importance in the community, I figure she wishes she'd let you marry him. She's always wanted to add Woodbeck Farm to ours and she muffed her only chance. I'm sure she wouldn't be nearly as opposed to your marriage as she once was."

"Thanks for telling me that, Summer, but the change in Nathan's social standing hasn't had any effect on me. I don't regard him more highly than I did when he was working for Daddy. I would have taken him when he was penniless."

The grandfather clock in the hall struck six o'clock, and as if on cue, the doorbell rang.

Autumn looked quizzically at Summer, who smiled mysteriously. "Mother doesn't give up easily, as you know. Don't blame me—I tried to dissuade her."

Mystified, Autumn walked into the dining room behind Summer and Dolly. Harrison Lowe, who was apparently also a dinner guest, was wheeling Clara into her place at the table.

Anger surged through Autumn until her ears rang, and she mustered all her willpower to keep back the denunciatory words that sprang to her lips. *Is she going to start this again? I won't stay. I can't allow Nathan to think I'm interested in Harrison.*

Trina gave her a warning glance, and Summer gripped the back of her chair. When she noted the surprise in Harrison's eyes, Autumn knew he hadn't been aware of Clara's scheme, either. She shouldn't take her anger out on him.

Harrison reached out a hand to her. "How nice to see you again, Autumn!"

She shook hands with him and introduced him to Dolly and Trina. *Did he remember the last time they'd sat together at this table? Had Harrison ever been interested in her as a prospective wife, or was the match only an idea in Clara's mind?*

Mrs. Hayes came into the dining room, followed by a maid. While the two women prepared to serve the food, Autumn wavered between leaving or staying, until an innocent remark from Dolly made her laugh, and she decided to deal with the dilemma the best she could.

With an appetizer of glazed pineapple hearts before them, Clara lifted her fork.

"Why, Mrs. Weaver!" Dolly said. "Are you going to eat without praying?"

Clara looked sharply at Dolly, and she said stiffly, "We're not accustomed to praying in this house!"

"Mama taught me never to eat without thanking God for my food." She folded her hands and closed her eyes. "God is great and God is good, and we thank Him for this food. Amen." Dolly opened her eyes, and with a bright smile, she said, "Now, we can eat."

Autumn exchanged an amused glance with Trina, but Dolly's unconscious gesture caused her anger to disappear. Trina was right. Anger wasn't going to change her mother, but love and prayer might. She resolved to act as if her mother had no ulterior motives for this dinner party. She was pleasant to her mother and Harrison.

They moved into the living room at the end of the meal, and Clara suggested that Autumn should take Dr. Lowe on a tour of the horse barns.

"Daddy is the one to do that," she refused. "I've been away from the horses too long. There's not much I can tell him."

At that opportune time, the beeper at Harrison's side sounded. He excused himself and went into the next room to take the call.

"I'm sorry to leave now," he said when he reentered the living room. "A hospital emergency." He bid them a cordial goodbye, and Summer walked to the door with him.

"He's certainly a gracious man," Clara said. "I can't imagine why his wife divorced him." With a pointed glance at Autumn, she said, "I suspect he'll remarry soon, since he has a child to raise."

"Mother," she said, "I have no interest in Harrison.

I believe the feeling is mutual. He's good company, and I've no doubt he's a fine doctor, but he isn't the man for me. I don't feel a tremor of excitement when he's around."

"I suppose Nathan Holland is exciting to you?"

Autumn smiled, remembering two nights ago when Nathan had kissed her and she'd felt as if the universe had exploded.

"He does have his exciting moments," she said. "Actually, how much do you know about Nathan? How many times have you talked with him?"

"I've never talked with him. My only contact with him has been at a distance."

"Then you really can't make a judgment on what Nathan is like. I don't know whether there'll ever be anything between us, but please leave us alone, Mother. Let us make that decision ourselves."

On the drive home, Trina said, "I thought the evening turned out well enough. And I'm proud of you for controlling your anger when you found out your mother had invited Dr. Lowe."

"I was angry," Autumn admitted, "but I didn't think I should take my frustrations out on Harrison. I'm sure he was an innocent party to the meeting. I only hope Nathan doesn't hear about the dinner."

Chapter Thirteen

But an incident the next day convinced Autumn that Nathan had heard about the dinner party. They were in surgery and Trina was monitoring the heartbeat of a sedated dachshund that had jumped over a fence and torn its stomach. The wound had been cleaned and Autumn was applying a few sutures when Olive entered the surgery. She closed the door behind her and waited until Autumn finished.

"Nathan is on the phone. He has another sick cow."

"Tell him I can come within a half hour," Autumn said, without lifting her eyes from the work she was doing.

Olive hesitated, before adding in a nervous voice, "He wants Trina to check on the animal. What shall I tell him?"

Autumn's head reeled. She closed her eyes and grabbed the table for support.

"I won't go," Trina said angrily.

"Yes, you will," Autumn responded grimly. "He

obviously doesn't want me, and we're obligated to take care of Ray's customers.''

"You're much better with large animals than I am."

"Makes no difference. I'll tell you what to do."

"I have to give him an answer," Olive insisted.

"I guess I'll have to go," Trina said. When Olive left the room, Trina tearfully said, "I'm so sorry about this. I thought you were getting along so well."

"I thought so, too. I suppose somehow he's learned that we had dinner with Dr. Lowe. He was jealous of my association with Harrison in the past." Her eyes blazed. "Will you tell me why I'm so fond of a man who doesn't trust me?"

The minute he hung up the phone, Nathan was sorry he'd asked for Trina. Maybe he'd jumped to the wrong conclusion again. Just because Autumn and Harrison had been invited to dinner at Indian Creek Farm didn't necessarily mean she was interested in him. And Jeff Smith, Weaver's horse trainer, had indicated that Trina and Dolly were there, too.

Leaning on the fence, watching his herd of Angus, while he waited for Trina, Nathan knew the trouble lay in the past. However hard he tried to throw off the feeling, he'd always felt inferior to the Weavers. To know that Dr. Lowe had been invited to dinner, while Autumn's parents wouldn't even acknowledge his existence hit him in his most vulnerable spot.

Landon had told him he wasn't good enough for his daughter, and at that time, Nathan agreed with him. He'd hoped that when he owned the adjoining farm to their own, the Weavers might be friendly. That hadn't happened. But in all honesty, he couldn't remember that Autumn had ever treated him as an inferior, so why did he take his frustrations out on her?

When he saw Autumn's car coming up the driveway, Nathan eagerly turned that way, happy that she'd come after all. She'd probably be as mad as an ornery bull, but he was prepared to deal with her anger and apologize. His spirits fell when Trina stepped out of the car.

She barely acknowledged his greeting.

"Where's the sick cow?" she asked in an icy voice.

He motioned toward the barn. During the next half hour, he watched as Trina quickly and efficiently applied the necessary treatment to the sick animal. She spoke only when she needed his help in some way. When she finished, she wrote out a statement for the call and medication and walked back to the car.

Silently, she got in the auto and drove several yards down the driveway. She stopped, stepped out of the car and walked back to where Nathan stood wondering what ailed Trina. Why was she so angry?

With brown eyes snapping, Trina said, "Autumn Weaver is the best friend I have, and I don't appreciate the way you treated her. As far as I'm concerned, your cow could have died, but she insisted that I make this call. Don't ask me to come again. Autumn is a better hand with livestock than I am, and if you want the best treatment for you cattle, you'd better have her."

Nathan felt like a little boy who'd been called on the carpet, and he flushed. "I guess I can call any vet I want to."

"That's right, as long as it isn't me. You hurt Autumn's feelings this morning, and I won't be a part of it."

Nathan stood, mouth agape as she hurried away,

jumped in the auto and drove rapidly toward the highway. He sat on the edge of the porch, his head in his hands. Should he apologize to Autumn? He remembered that as a girl Autumn was sensitive—her feelings easily hurt. Why did he always make the wrong decisions with Autumn?

Business at the clinic was brisk for the next two days, and every afternoon, Autumn went on calls that took her far away from Greensboro, even to neighboring counties, and she didn't get home until late. She couldn't understand Nathan's treatment of her. When she'd taken a picnic to him, he'd kissed her and gave all the impressions of loving her. They'd had an enjoyable time at the auction. Why had he suddenly gotten angry at her? She had to find out.

Thursday evening, after not hearing from Nathan again for six days, she drove past Nathan's farm about seven o'clock. Figuring that Nathan would have been driven in from the fields by several afternoon showers, Autumn slowed as she approached his driveway, reluctant to drive in. What if he rejected her again?

She was at the crossroads—which way would she go? Momentarily she considered flipping a coin. Heads, I stop to see Nathan; tails, I let him make the next move. She prayed instead. *God, help me know what to do. I don't mind paying for my past sins against Nathan, but haven't I suffered enough?*

She lifted her foot from the brake pedal and turned into Nathan's driveway. His pickup was parked beside the barn, so he must be at home. She'd try the house first. As she stepped up on the back porch, she sniffed tempting aromas from the gas grill beside the door.

She peered through the screen door into the kitchen where Nathan stood at the sink chopping vegetables. Had he heard her drive in and was ignoring her?

Knocking, she said, "Hi. Got any extra food for a hungry woman? The meat on the grill sure smells good."

His hands hovered momentarily over the food he was preparing before he turned. Without smiling, he said, "Come in, Autumn. I can throw an extra hamburger on the grill. Or do you want more than one?"

"I was really joking. I didn't mean to interrupt your supper. I'll wait on the porch until you've finished."

He reached in the refrigerator and brought out a hamburger patty, stepped out on the porch and placed it on the grill. "You might as well try some of this hamburger. It's from one of my own beeves. I picked it up from the meat packer this afternoon."

He held the door open for her, and she stepped inside.

"Okay, if it's not too much trouble. I haven't eaten since morning. This has been a busy day. In fact, the whole week has been hectic. I don't know how Ray handles all this work by himself, but I'll find out in a few weeks. Trina has to take Dolly back to her mother before Ray comes home, so I told her she didn't need to come back."

"I understand she's getting married soon," Nathan said as he set out several bottles of salad dressing, put two bowls of salad on the table and lifted a bubbling pot of corn chowder from the oven.

"In December. Her fiancé is a vet student and they'll set up a practice together when he finishes his studies."

Nathan brought the grilled hamburgers from the

porch, placed a plate for Autumn, sat down opposite her, bowed his head and said a short blessing. They didn't talk much while they ate, for now that she was with Nathan, Autumn didn't know how to approach him. Nathan had hardly looked at her, and she thought her presence made him nervous. When they finished, Nathan brought cups and poured coffee for them. He set a sack of cookies on the table.

Grinning, he said, "My bakery products come from the deli. I don't mind cooking, but I don't like to bake, even if I had the time." He pushed back from the table, propped one leg on his knee and seemed to relax as he drank the coffee. Autumn was far from relaxed. What should she say?

"What are you going to do when Ray gets back? He's been looking for an assistant."

"So Miss Olive keeps telling me," Autumn said, with a wry grin. "I've been considering it, but my decision depends on a lot of things."

He looked at her questioningly, but said nothing. His cool attitude wasn't helping her. Although Nathan had been polite enough, she felt like an unwanted guest, and that the sooner she left, the happier he'd be.

"Do you think a person can bury the past and start over again?" she asked.

"Sure. I have. I've overcome the stigma of being fired from Indian Creek Farm and have finally been accepted in the community as a progressive farmer."

If Nathan had intended to hurt her with his comment, he'd succeeded. How could she forget the past when he'd just dumped the whole episode in her lap again?

"If you'll excuse me, Autumn, I still have some work to take care of before dark."

"Is there anything I can help with?"

"No, thanks."

She was discouraged by his impassive face and lack of response. If she could only tell what he was thinking. It was obvious that he wanted her to leave.

"Can't you give me a little more of your time? I didn't stop here tonight for a free meal. I want to know why you suddenly preferred Trina's work to mine."

He didn't hesitate a minute before he flung his answer at her. "A case of the past repeating itself, I suppose. I heard about the dinner party at Indian Creek Farm a few nights ago. I didn't know you and Dr. Lowe were seeing each other."

"Mother invited me to come for dinner, without telling me that Dr. Lowe was going to be there. We sat at the same table and ate, but I hardly consider that 'seeing each other.'"

He left the table, leaned against the sink and faced her with eyes that were unfriendly or unconcerned? She couldn't tell.

"Perhaps I'm in the wrong. But when Jeff Smith stopped by and mentioned that you and Dr. Lowe had come to the farm for dinner, all I could think about was the other time you'd been so friendly to me and started me dreaming about you. And the first thing I knew you were going to marry the doctor."

"I never planned to marry Dr. Lowe. How many times do I have to tell you that? It seems to me that you still haven't forgiven me for what happened eight years ago."

"I told you when you came back to Greensboro that I'd forgiven you a long time ago."

"But have you *forgotten?* I've heard people say, 'I forgive, but I can't forget.' Can't you forget your suspicions of what happened between Dr. Lowe and me? Let's forget the past and start over."

He wouldn't meet her eyes, and he turned his back and started scrubbing on the bowl that had held the chowder.

"I told you I'd overcome the past and started over."

"You're not making this easy for me, Nathan. When I say bury the past, I mean I want us to be friends."

"I consider you a friend, Autumn."

Here they were sparring again, but this time it wasn't amusing!

Sighing, Autumn said, "I can't seem to give up easily. I wonder why I didn't get any of the Weaver pride Mother talks about, but I'll continue to grovel and say it plainly. I'm not content to be just a friend, Nathan. Time has changed many things, but not that, and I'll always believe, whether you admit it or not, that you once felt the same way about me. When I said that my remaining in Greensboro depends on many things, I meant us, Nathan. *Us!* If you'll open your heart to me, I'll stay as Ray's assistant. Otherwise, I'll set up my practice elsewhere. The call is up to you. Where do we go from here?"

Nathan gripped the edge of the sink and stared out the window where his prized Angus cattle grazed in the lush meadow. Why did he have trouble believing that she really meant what she said? Did he have an inferiority complex that kept him from accepting the fact that Autumn Weaver really wanted him?

He heard her chair push away from the table, and he turned toward her.

"I guess you've given me my answer, Nathan. I won't bother you again."

She paused with her hand on the door latch when he spoke. "If I make a success of this farm, I have to devote my full time to it. I work more than fifteen hours a day, and I'm operating on a limited budget. I have neither the time nor the money to pursue a relationship with anyone. I don't want to be the cause of your refusal to take a position in Ray's clinic because it seems the right place for you. We've gotten along all right this summer meeting on an impersonal basis. Why can't we continue that way?"

More than anything, he wanted her to stay, for to lose her again would be unbearable.

"No. I don't consider it impersonal, and I won't have my heart trampled on again. I've tried to make restitution for what I did to you eight years ago, but you won't meet me halfway. When I leave Greensboro this time, my conscience will be clear, for I've done all I can do. I pray I can start a new life and find happiness elsewhere."

He came to her side and turned her to face him. "Do you think you're the only one with a trampled heart? To me, you were like a goddess on a pedestal, and I didn't think I was worthy to wipe your shoes. I agreed with your father about that. I knew I wasn't good enough for you. But you toppled off that pedestal when you wouldn't defend me to your father. The day I drove away from Indian Creek Farm, I made up my mind I'd never trust anyone else with my heart."

"Because of a decision you made then, you still won't trust me? Even now, you think I'm playacting, that I only want you to prove I can have what I want?

You didn't believe I could care about you before, and you still don't.''

He went to the fireplace and took a picture off the mantel. "You wanted to know why I bought the frame at the auction. I wanted it for this photograph.''

She was suddenly weak-kneed when she saw her own face staring back from the frame. Nathan explained how he'd come into possession of her picture. "I've had it hidden away for years, but after the past few weeks, I thought it was time to put it on display. Now, I wonder.''

Autumn's heartbeat thumped in her side knowing that he'd treasured her photograph all of these years, but she was too emotionally drained now to consider the impact of it.

She walked to the porch, and he followed her. At the bottom of the steps, she stopped and looked up at him.

"I came here with several goals in mind. I wanted to bury the past and I'm grateful I've accomplished that. I wanted to ask your forgiveness. You say you've forgiven me, and I'll accept that. My aspirations for the future are gone, and I'll accept that, too. I'll leave as soon as Ray returns. In the meantime, if we have another conversation, you'll initiate it.''

"Autumn, wait…'' Nathan said, but she ran to the pickup and drove away without speaking again.

Nathan dropped into the old rocking chair, where his uncle had spent so much time viewing his farm. Sight of the acres that usually thrilled him brought no peace of mind to Nathan now. He hardly noticed the tranquil setting where Beauty grazed along a little stream that flowed into Indian Creek.

Had he lost his mind? Autumn had offered herself

to him again, and he'd turned her down just as he'd done before. Wasn't it a sign of insanity for a man to reject the woman he'd dreamed about for years—the only woman he'd ever wanted? At one time he'd believed she was only flirting with him, but he didn't believe that now. At eighteen, she'd been spoiled and willful—and desirable, too, he had to admit. She wanted him in spite of her parents' displeasure, and it was plain enough that she was still of the same persuasion. She said she didn't have any Weaver pride, but he knew she did have, and he realized it must have been difficult for her to approach him tonight.

She had enough Weaver pride that he doubted he could win her now even if he wanted to. Did he want Autumn? *God, You know I do, so why am I hesitating? Why did You bring us back together after all of this time? I've got only a few weeks to know if she's the woman for me.*

His farm chores forgotten, Nathan sat on the porch until long after midnight wondering what he could do to keep Autumn in the neighborhood long enough for them to discover if they shared enough love to last for a lifetime.

Still smarting from Nathan's treatment, Autumn tried to hide her dismay from Trina and the others. The next day was Dolly's seventh birthday and Trina planned a celebration for her. They invited Miss Olive to accompany them to a restaurant in the shopping mall that specialized in Chinese food, Dolly's favorite meal. Believing that a good appearance might make up for her lack of gaiety, Autumn stopped by the beauty shop for a haircut and shampoo, giving the beautician strict orders that her hair must stay shoulder-length. If she was through with Nathan, why did she let him dictate her hairstyle? She dressed in a white silk blouse and dark navy skirt. They'd just ordered when Autumn's portable phone rang. An excited voice sounded in her ear.

"Okay, I'll be there as soon as possible." To Trina, she said, "One of the Simpson racehorses may have a broken leg. If you'll leave long enough to drive me to the clinic, you can come back and enjoy the meal." She hugged Dolly and handed her a wrapped package. "Sorry, I can't stay and celebrate. Enjoy your gift."

Trina dropped her off at the clinic and Autumn hurried to Ray's truck. She didn't take time to change her clothes, but headed out of town on a graveled road that brought her to the Simpson farm in fifteen minutes. Sandy came running around the side of the barn, with Tony and Debbie at her heels.

"Oh, Autumn, can you help us? Ralph is away for overnight, and I don't know what to do." She tried to calm Tony and Debbie when they started crying.

"Please, Sandy, calm yourself. I'll do what I can. What happened?" She pulled a pair of Ray's coveralls over her skirt.

Sandy motioned to her son. "Tony was riding the colt around the paddock when a covey of quail flew out of the bushes. That scared the horse, and he struck his right foreleg on the fence when he reared and threw Tony to the ground. I think the leg is broken." Tears streamed down her full-moon face.

"Where is the colt?"

"In the paddock behind the barn," Tony said.

The colt was still on his feet, but the panic-stricken Thoroughbred wouldn't let Autumn get near him. The injured leg flopped around when the animal moved.

Observing at a distance, Autumn thought it was possible the break was a minor one, but if the horse continued walking on the leg, he could suffer irreparable damage. Autumn couldn't bear to think of such a beautiful animal having to be put down.

"Do you have a hired hand or someone else who can help me?" she asked.

Sandy shook her head. "Our farm worker has gone for the day, and he lives on the other side of Greensboro."

"I can help," Tony said.

Autumn refused Tony's offer. She needed adult assistance and the nearest help was at Woodbeck Farm. Momentarily, forgetting their estrangement when they'd parted before, and without even wondering if he'd refuse, Autumn got her phone from the truck and dialed Nathan's number. The phone rang seven times, and she was almost ready to hang up when he answered.

"Oh, Nathan, I'm so glad you're home. I'm at the Simpson farm, and their Thoroughbred colt has a broken leg. Ralph is gone, and I need some help to restrain the animal."

"I'll be there in a few minutes."

Chapter Fourteen

By the time Autumn had put on coveralls, gotten medications, a twitch and a set of hobbles from the truck, she heard a vehicle racing up the driveway. Nathan pulled his truck to a stop beside hers and took the hobbles from her hands.

"The horse is in the paddock," she said, and hurried in that direction with Nathan at her side. She explained what had happened. "Sandy is beside herself."

"I don't blame her. Ralph paid over ten thousand dollars for that colt. I've helped Ralph work him a few times, so he may not be afraid of me. I'll give it a try."

Sandy and the two kids were trying to coax the colt to come to them.

"Sandy," Nathan said, "the best way you can help is to get out of the paddock and take Debbie and Tony with you. Autumn and I will do all that needs to be done. Go to the house and try to locate Ralph. He needs to know about this."

Reluctantly, Sandy moved away, and Debbie went with her, but Tony lingered outside the fence, his freckled face lined with worry.

"Let me watch, Mr. Holland. I won't be a bother."

Nathan nodded as he slowly approached the frightened animal, carrying the twitch, a valuable device for restraining animals. The Thoroughbred shied away from him, but he soon succeeded in placing his hand on its neck and patted it a few times before he slipped the chain loop of the twitch over the horse's upper lip and twisted until it was tight. He nodded to Autumn, who approached the colt slowly and knelt to run capable hands over the animal's leg. When she touched the sore spot, the animal snorted, and Nathan quickly tightened the twitch.

"It's broken, but it seems like a clean break. I'll numb the leg and give him a tranquilizer to keep him quiet. Can you help me put him on the ground by using the rope and hobbles?"

"Just tell me what you want done."

After the injection temporarily dulled the pain in the leg, the colt was easier to handle. Autumn placed a belly band on the animal, put hobbles on its back legs, and threaded a rope from one hobble through the belly band down to the other hobble and gave the rope to Nathan, who was still restraining the animal with the twitch.

"Remove the twitch now and help me lower him to the ground. It really isn't difficult if the hobbles are on correctly, and I believe they are."

Slowly they eased the colt to the ground and tied his legs in a flexed position. Once they had the animal so he couldn't harm himself, Autumn knelt on the ground and made a more thorough examination. Her blue eyes were troubled when she looked at Nathan, who stooped near the horse's head.

"There's definitely a fracture. I'm sure the break can be repaired so the horse won't be lame, but it's a job I can't handle. I've watched this procedure, but I'm not a surgeon."

"There's an excellent equine orthopedic surgeon in Columbus."

Sandy ran around the side of the barn, phone in hand. "I've got Ralph on the phone," she said. "He wants to talk to you, Autumn."

She took the phone from Sandy. Ralph's worried tones sounded in her ear. "What can you tell me?"

"We've tranquilized the animal and he's restrained so he won't damage himself, but there's a fracture of the right foreleg. If we take him to a surgeon immediately, I believe he has a fifty-fifty chance of complete recovery. Nathan is here with me. He says there's an equine surgeon in Columbus."

"Is that what you recommend?"

"If it was my horse, I'd take him to the surgeon. I don't have the training nor the experience to handle this situation."

"Let me talk to Nathan then?"

Autumn handed the phone to Nathan and he listened to Ralph's concerns.

"I agree with Autumn," Nathan said. "Except for the break, the colt is okay."

He listened again. "Call back in ten minutes. I'll see if we can contact the surgeon in Columbus. If he's available, I'll arrange to take your horse to Columbus, and you can meet us there."

To Autumn, he said, "I'll have to look up the surgeon's address and number, and I'll telephone from the house. We should find a padded trailer to take the horse to Columbus. If Sandy telephones your father, he'll probably loan her his trailer."

While Nathan made these arrangements, Autumn sat beside the restless colt, and monitored the heartbeat occasionally. Debbie and Tony stayed with Autumn and patted the horse's side.

"Poor horsey," Debbie said. "He's hurt bad."

"That's true," Autumn agreed, "but he'll probably be all right."

"You'll make him well just like you did Flossie."

Autumn laughed slightly. "This is a more difficult break than what Flossie had, but I'm sure the surgeon in Columbus can fix him up in a hurry."

Nathan's expression was encouraging when he returned. He hunkered down beside Autumn. "It's all taken care of. The surgeon will be waiting for us. Sandy said your father willingly loaned his trailer, and two men from Indian Creek Farm will be here shortly to help us. They're bringing a hoist so we can move the horse into the trailer. I'll ride along and keep an eye on him." To Tony, he said, "Help me move a few of these fence panels so the trailer can drive into the paddock."

As Autumn watched Nathan take charge, she compared him to what he'd been when she'd first met him. Then, he was unsure of himself, suffered from low self-esteem, and had no prospects for the future. Now he was strong, assured and capable. The young man she'd admired was even more appealing and desirable now. Nathan's eyes met hers and held for a few brief moments. As if he could read her thoughts, he started toward her, paused and turned away.

To hide her confusion, she got some medication and

explained its purpose to Nathan in case the horse started thrashing around in the trailer.

"You've done a good job on this, Autumn."

"I wish I could have done more."

"Having the courage to admit you lack expertise in this situation probably saved the horse for a productive future. A more opinionated vet might have fiddled around with the leg, tried to set it on his own, which might have worked, but if it hadn't, it would have been too late for surgery. You've done a great job, in my opinion."

Dropping her gaze, she said, "Thanks. Your opinion is important to me."

He ignored Debbie and Tony, who looked on with interest, and drew Autumn into his arms. She shivered in his embrace, and he massaged her back.

"Thanks for coming, Nathan. Considering our last meeting, I shouldn't have called you, but you were the first person I thought of. I didn't know what to do."

"Remember you're a Weaver. You can't fail at anything."

His words hurt, for as a child she'd heard them too often from Clara. She tried to pull away from him, but his arms tightened.

"Let me go. I can't take any ridicule tonight."

"I wasn't ridiculing you. There are times when I resent the way the Weavers have treated me, but I respect their abilities and self-confidence."

She surrendered to the comfort of his embrace a few more seconds, and he ruffled her hair.

"I see you've had a haircut."

"Just a little. My hair grows so fast, I have to keep it under control."

Her head was still on his shoulder, but she sensed

amusement in his voice. "I was only teasing. I'd like you if you cut off all your hair." His tone changed. "Autumn, try to forget the things I said last night. It's a sore spot with me that while I grew up in near-poverty conditions, you were living at Indian Creek Farm. I still find it difficult to believe that you want me for your—" he hesitated "—your friend."

"The trailer's coming, Mr. Holland," Tony shouted, and Nathan released her, but not before he left a soft kiss on her trembling lips.

It was dark by then, but the security light illuminated the area as the truck backed into the paddock where the horse lay.

Autumn recognized the driver as Jeff Smith, who had come to work for her father shortly before she left home. Jeff shook hands with her, and since she knew her father would have trained him sufficiently, she asked Jeff to take charge of loading the colt. Autumn and Nathan followed Jeff's instructions as they hoisted the injured animal into the trailer. Sandy came from the house with two thermoses of coffee and a sack of sandwiches.

"Here's something for you to snack on while you travel. Ralph and I are grateful for what you're doing for us. Nathan, tell Ralph to call me as soon as the surgery is over."

Nathan climbed into the trailer, covered the sedated horse with a couple of blankets and sat down.

"I might take a nap, too," he said with a grin. He lifted a hand, and his eyes connected with Autumn's until she closed the trailer's rear gate. Tony and Debbie ran beside the trailer until it picked up speed and headed toward Columbus.

Sandy took Autumn's hand. "Let's have a prayer

for them." She bowed her head. "Thank you, God, for those who've come to our aid tonight. Thanks for sending Autumn to Greensboro and for her knowledge. I'm grateful for good neighbors, too. Keep all of them safe as they travel. Amen."

She helped Autumn gather her equipment and carry it to the truck. "Come in for a cup of coffee," she said.

"I'll settle for a cup of hot tea and a sandwich. I was just getting ready to sit down for dinner when your call came. My hands and legs are shaky, and I don't think it's safe for me to drive home until I have a little nourishment."

"I've still got the fixings out from the sandwiches I made for the men. What'll you have—balogna, cheese, ham, turkey?"

"A slice each of balogna and cheese, please. A little mayonnaise."

"White or brown bread?"

"Brown."

When they entered the kitchen, Sandy said, "There's a washroom around the corner."

Before she washed, Autumn took off the coveralls, and when she went back in the kitchen, Sandy said, "I see you're dressed up. I hope my call didn't interrupt an important engagement."

"We were treating Dolly to Chinese food for her birthday, but she's been around us enough to know that we have to take care of the calls," Autumn said. She eased slowly into a chair by the kitchen table to rest her wobbly legs. Reaction was setting in now that she had time to dwell on the serious condition of the horse, her appeal to Nathan and his response. His public kiss had climaxed a traumatic evening. That kiss hadn't come from a man who feared to trust his heart to her. All of these things had happened too fast, and she needed time to sort everything out in her mind.

Sandy sat opposite Autumn and sipped on a cup of coffee. The kitchen was clean, but it was cluttered with toys, video games, farming magazines and an assortment of dishes and pans on the cabinets. Comparing it to the tidy Weaver house of her youth, Autumn decided that the Simpsons had a *home* rather than a *house*. She liked it. For a moment, she allowed herself to envision the house at Woodbeck Farm, wondering if she'd ever have an opportunity to make a home for Nathan and herself there.

Normally a chatterer, Sandy was even more talkative tonight because of her worry over the Thoroughbred. Lost in her own musings, Autumn had missed much of what she said, but she did owe it to Sandy to forget her own problems for a while.

"This sandwich is good, Sandy. Just what I needed for the strength to get back to town."

"I hate to be nosy, Autumn, but you and Nathan seem to be more friendly than when you first returned to Greensboro. What happened to you in the past?"

Autumn's hand shook, and she laid down the rest of her sandwich. She couldn't meet Sandy's eyes.

"Forgive me," Sandy said. "Eat your sandwich and forget I said that."

Autumn picked up the sandwich and nibbled on it. The contents didn't taste nearly as good as they had before.

"I knew Nathan for about six months before I left Greensboro eight years ago. He worked for my father, and I made a fool of myself over him," Autumn said bluntly, not sparing herself. "My father found out we'd been seeing each other and he fired Nathan. When Nathan left town, I ran away, too, for my mother was trying to promote a romance between me and Dr. Lowe to counteract my interest in Nathan. If Doc Wheeler had told me Nathan was back in this neighborhood, I wouldn't have come to be his helper this summer.''

Sandy's eyes had widened, and she'd listened to Autumn, mouth agape.

"I'm surprised you hadn't heard. I thought everyone in the county knew the whole story.''

"We didn't buy this farm until a year ago, and although we've met Mr. Weaver often, I've never felt free to call at Indian Creek Farm because of your mother's health. I've never met Mrs. Weaver or your sister. It was obvious when you came into our Sunday school class, that there was something between you and Nathan. I'd never seen him so flustered.''

"It was a mistake for me to come back. My father won't speak to me, and Mother is unforgiving. I'd leave now, but I feel obligated to stay and fulfill my commitment to Ray. I'm sure he thought he'd help out the situation by asking me to come back, but if anything, it's worse. I'd learned to live alone, and when I leave in a few weeks, it's going to be difficult to part with everything I love a second time.''

"Nathan still seems to be interested in you. Why leave?''

"That's a decision I'll have to make when Ray returns," Autumn replied as she pushed back from the table. "Thanks for the food, but I must get back to town. I'm sure Trina is wondering what happened.''

Sandy walked to the truck with her and put her arm around Autumn's shoulder for a quick squeeze.

"Don't think your return to Greensboro has been a complete disaster. If it hadn't been for you, we might have had to put our horse down. God brought you home for a reason, and I pray you'll find the peace and happiness you deserve."

It was nearing midnight when Autumn pulled into the garage on the Wheeler property. A light burned in the kitchen, and when she stepped up on the back porch, Trina spoke from the swing.

"How did it go?"

Autumn sat beside her and as they swung slowly, she said, "It's been a strange situation." She related the dramatic events of the evening.

"And you think the animal can be saved?"

"There's a good chance, he will be. You remember some of the successful surgeries we watched when we were in training. The Simpson horse is in better shape than most of those, so I'm hopeful. Nathan says the surgeon is capable."

"Do you think what happened tonight will have an effect on the relationship between you and Nathan?"

Autumn sighed. "I'm foolish enough to think so. He was so self-assured as he helped me, not at all like the bewildered youth I used to know. And he was tender with me, almost as if he really cared for me. I've relived every minute of what he said and did tonight, and I do think there's some hope."

"I think so, too. Both of you need to forget the past."

"You don't have to convince me. I've been waiting a long time for that to happen."

They swung back and forth companionably, such close friends that they didn't need to talk.

* * *

The ringing phone awakened Autumn at six o'clock the next morning. She reached for the phone, hoping it was Sandy reporting on the injured horse, but it could just as well be a farmer with an urgent need.

"Hello, Autumn, sorry if I awakened you." Autumn sat up, suddenly alert. It was Nathan, not Sandy, calling.

"Where are you, Nathan? What do you know?"

He answered her second question first. "The surgeon thinks the operation was successful, and that the colt will be able to run competitively by the time he's old enough. He wants to keep him for a couple of days, so Ralph and I came home. We just got here."

"Thanks for calling right away. I've been restless all night wondering what was happening."

"The surgeon was complimentary of how you'd handled the situation, so you deserve a lot of credit, too."

"Thanks! I'll bet you're tired."

"I'm still excited that we could save the animal, but I'm going to bed for a few hours."

"Goodbye, Nathan, and thanks again."

"Are you coming to work on the cart tonight? The fair is next week."

He apparently intended to ignore their heated words during her last visit to his farm.

"Yes, I'll come about seven o'clock. If you're busy with farm work, I'll work alone."

Autumn left her bed. She was excited and more optimistic about the future than she'd been for a long time.

Chapter Fifteen

The renovation of the cart progressed steadily, and the night before the opening of the county fair, Autumn went to Woodbeck Farm for last minute touch-ups on the paint. Nathan was standing on a stool, grooming Beauty and trying to braid her mane in the acceptable manner for showing.

"I can't get the hang of this," he complained, as he jerked on the ribbons he was trying to braid into Beauty's mane. "I must not have done it right, for she's been fretting. I can't show her this way."

"Is this the first time you've braided her mane?" Autumn asked.

"I've practiced it several times. Always before, I managed. I'm nervous tonight, since tomorrow is my first competition. It's not easy to be competing against the Weavers."

Would he ever get over the wound her family had inflicted on his self-esteem?

"Don't forget there'll be one Weaver cheering for you tomorrow!"

He nodded. "And I appreciate it, too."

Beauty's head was secured to a wall in an awkward position, which could be causing the filly's uneasiness.

"It takes a long while before animals get used to braiding, and they don't like it at first. Let me see what I can do. I did the braiding on Daddy's horses for several years."

"Help yourself," Nathan said, stepping off the stool. "I haven't practiced enough apparently."

"Help me lower her head a bit. She seems uncomfortable."

When they had the filly's head in a more satisfactory position, Autumn stepped up on the braiding stool and brushed out the braid Nathan had tried. She turned Beauty's mane to the right side, laying the mane roll over the filly's neck. Using blue and white ribbons, she tied the white ribbon around the rolls not far from the end. Autumn faced in the same way the mare faced. Starting two inches back of the ears, she selected a strand of hair, equal to one strand of the mane roll, separated it from the rest of the mane and held it upright. She crossed the ribbon behind the strand of hair.

At first, Autumn's fingers fumbled, for it had been a long time since she'd decorated the Weaver horses, but soon the skill returned. She quickly and artfully continued crossing the ribbon and hair in the same order until she had the mane prepared in the commonly used Aberdeen Plait. She evenly spaced five flowers in the mane, and stepped off the stool to survey her work.

"I thought I might have forgotten how to do that," she said.

Nathan admired her work with glowing eyes. "That's a masterpiece of work."

Autumn's face beamed with satisfaction as she flexed her fingers. "I'll have sore hands tomorrow, but it will be worth the pain. Let me braid the tail, too, please."

"Go ahead," Nathan agreed heartily.

"I'll braid the Scotch Knot on her tail," Autumn told Nathan. "That's faster."

Autumn picked up the raffia from a table and prepared the two stick-ups for the tail, then she proceeded to use a four-plait braid, two strands of hair and two of raffia. She checked to be sure the two stick-ups were even in height and square across the tail. When the stick-ups were braided and wrapped tightly into a small fan shape, she arranged the tail in an ordinary three-plait braid. She ended by placing a narrow ribbon bow on the stick-up at the base of the fan and stood back to survey her work.

"That looks wonderful, Autumn. Thanks."

"Thank *you* for letting me help you. This was only a practice session, but it's good to know I haven't forgotten how to decorate horses," Autumn said with gratification. "I'll be at the fair grounds tomorrow in time to get her ready for showing," she said, patting the Belgian's broad rump.

Nathan had marveled at Autumn's dexterity. He'd failed to appreciate Autumn in the past. The woman had a rare skill with horses, a trait inherited from the Weavers before her. He couldn't understand why her father was so unforgiving, unwilling to bring her home to give him the help he needed. But on the other hand, was he any different from Landon Weaver? He kept rebuffing Autumn, when it was obvious what a tremendous helpmate she'd be for any man who wanted to raise and show draft horses.

Autumn stood on the stool and put her arms around Beauty's neck. "She's well-named. She is a beauty. I hope you win."

After securing Beauty in a stall, Nathan said, "Come sit on the porch before you leave. What do you want to drink?"

"A cola sounds good."

Twilight fell around them as they sat in two huge rockers.

"I've promised Dolly that we'll spend the whole day at the fair. She's a nice kid, and I'll miss her when Trina takes her back to Wisconsin. Trina's fiancé is coming to collect them next week."

Nathan took her glass and set it beside his on the wicker table beside his chair. The stillness of the night was broken by the creak of their rockers as they weaved back and forth in rhythm and by the low bawl of a calf and the cacophony of myriad insects.

Nathan moved his chair closer to Autumn and reached for her hand. "At first, you were sorry you'd come home. What about now?"

He caressed her hand with his strong fingers, and she lifted both of their hands together and kissed his, wondering how such a powerful hand could be so comforting.

"No. I'm not sorry I came home."

They sat in silence, savoring the quietness and coolness of the night, enjoying being together. When she reluctantly made a move to leave, Nathan walked to the car with her.

"I'm happy you came back to Greensboro, too. My memories of you were fading. I'd almost forgotten how much I enjoyed being with you. It's like meeting you for the first time. I mentioned several days ago that God wants us to look to the future rather than the past. I'm beginning to think it's not only possible, but God's will for us to make a new beginning.''

Her pulse raced, and she searched his eyes in the soft glow from the dusk-to-dawn light, observing the same yearning she felt. He wants me, she thought, but he's afraid. He's reluctant to risk being hurt again. God willing, she'd never disappoint him, but how could he know that?

''I don't know why not,'' she said evenly, although she was ready to bridge the gap in one quick leap. Her heart cried out, we've only got a few more weeks, but she couldn't rush him this time. She had to give him time to learn he could trust her.

Nathan kissed her long and ardently, whispering terms of endearment he'd dreamed of saying during the years they'd been separated. Releasing her was one of the hardest things he'd ever done. He wanted to keep her with him forever, but now wasn't the time to tell her so. He opened the car door, and after she started the engine, he leaned in the open window and kissed her again.

Nathan's caresses had done wonders for Autumn's confidence, and she dared to believe that she and Nathan, like the mythical phoenix, could build a future on the ashes of their past mistakes.

That night Ray telephoned from Israel, and Autumn was surprised to hear his voice when she answered.

''Hi. How are things going?'' he asked.

''More than you'd want to hear over the telephone. And by the way, I have a quarrel to pick with you!

You got me back to Greensboro under false pretenses," she accused.

"Not at all," Ray protested. "Everything I told you was true."

"But it's what you didn't tell me that caused the problem. Would you believe that my first call was to Woodbeck Farm, and I had no idea about the change in ownership until I encountered Nathan out in his pasture? You're one of the few people who knew how I felt about Nathan, so you should have forewarned me."

"If I'd told you he was living in the neighborhood, would you have returned?

"Probably not."

"That's the reason I didn't tell you. How are things working out between you and Nathan? And with your parents? I hate seeing people I like and respect being miserable. This seemed like a good opportunity to get you back together. Has it worked?"

"I've only seen Daddy once when he passed me on the street and wouldn't speak to me. Mother has demanded my presence at the farm twice when Daddy was away, but she's still angry at me. As for Nathan, I'm beginning to hope."

"The summer isn't over yet."

"When will you be back?"

"A little longer than we'd expected, but we're scheduled to return to Chicago in three weeks. Do you think you can hang on until then?"

"What other choice do I have?"

"None," he said, with a laugh. "Let me talk to Olive. I'll see you in a few weeks."

Ray's telephone call had alerted Autumn, and she wasn't sleepy. She got into bed and picked up her

Bible. Turning on the radio beside her bed, she listened to the words of a song she hadn't heard before.

If our memories would span the past,
And keep love's light aglow;
Would they build a bridge of love,
So the future we might know?

Was love the only thing that could bridge the wide chasm separating her from the people she loved? Autumn's knowledge of the Bible was still scanty, but in her most desperate days during the separation from her family, she had learned to rely for comfort on the words from Paul's writings, often referred to as the Love chapter in the Apostle's first letter to the Corinthians.

Love is patient, love is kind. It does not envy, it does not boast, it is not proud. It is not rude, it is not self-seeking, it is not easily angered, it keeps no record of wrongs. Love does not delight in evil but rejoices with the truth. It always protects, always trusts, always hopes, always perseveres. Love never fails.

She sincerely believed that she had enough of that kind of love for her parents and Nathan to build the bridge that would join them together, but she could only build part of the structure. The loved ones she'd wronged would have to meet her halfway.

Autumn had read the newspapers during the weeks she'd been at the clinic, always pleased with the occasional news that the Belgian horses from Indian

Creek Farm had won many trophies. She had no doubt that the Weaver horses would be big winners at the fair today, but she did hope Nathan would receive some recognition.

When she and Dolly entered the fairgrounds, Autumn glanced nostalgically at the covered tents and trailers of the food vendors, at the excited children who ran from one exhibit to another, and at the 4-H members grooming their animals for showing. Music wafting from the carnival area invigorated her steps as she pointed out to Dolly all the pleasures she'd once enjoyed.

She avoided the area where the Weaver horses were being groomed for competition. Checking the schedule, and noting that Nathan would be showing in a couple of hours, Autumn said, "Let's see if we can find Nathan. I've promised to help him prepare Beauty."

"All right," Dolly said. "Will I be allowed to pet your daddy's big horses?"

"Not today. You'll have to content yourself with petting Beauty. It's better if we don't bother the others while they're getting ready for competition, but Nathan won't mind our company."

Autumn didn't know how much Dolly understood about the problem with her parents. She and Trina had never discussed the situation in Dolly's presence, but the girl was intelligent. She picked up more than they expected.

"That's all right," Dolly agreed. "I like Mr. Holland."

Tony Simpson was helping Nathan, and they'd spaced themselves a good distance from the Weaver operations. Nathan was gently smoothing the filly's glossy coat with a curry comb.

"Hi, Mr. Holland. We came to watch you in the show." Dolly shouted when she saw him.

He looked up and smiled at Dolly, but his eyes met Autumn's, and she noted the concern in his gaze.

"Good. I'll need all the support I can get. I'm getting nervous."

"You shouldn't be," Autumn assured him. "That cart is as acceptable as the expensive one Daddy has, and Beauty looks great. As soon as I get the braiding finished, she'll be in the same class as any Weaver horse. And I'm not telling you that to make you feel good. I mean it."

"Next to your father, I'd trust your judgment about draft horses more than anyone else. That's not what worries me. The horse's performance depends on the driver. I'm not sure I'm capable of handling her." He looked directly in her eyes. "I don't want to make a botch of this before your father. I'd like to do something that would cause him to respect me."

Autumn realized that her father's denunciation of him as an individual and a prospective suitor for her had wounded Nathan deeply. She found it hard to forgive her father for that. Was that why Nathan hesitated to resume their relationship? Did he still want to earn Landon Weaver's respect and permission before he claimed his daughter?

"Forget Daddy for the moment. All you have to do when you're competing is to win the approval of the judges. I have confidence in you. You'll be great in showmanship."

"I hate to ask you because you've already been such a help, but will you do me another favor, Autumn? I'd like for you and Dolly to ride with me in the cart. If you're with me, I won't feel so alone."

Dolly clapped her hands. "Let's do, Autumn. That sounds like a lot of fun."

Autumn wondered how it would affect her father to see her riding with the man he disliked and resented, but she had to consider Nathan now. Once she'd turned from him to stay with her father. She wouldn't put Nathan in second place again. She looked down at her jeans and blue-plaid shirt.

"I'm not dressed in the Weaver tradition for competition, and that seat is a little short for three people, but why not? I'd love to, Nathan."

"I'd let you drive if I wasn't registered in the men's division. You'd do a better job than I will."

She shook her head. "Not with a horse I haven't handled much. The driver has to know the mare and she has to know you. But Dolly and I will ride along."

Nathan handed Tony five dollars. "Tony, you and Dolly go buy something to eat and drink. Autumn needs to concentrate on what she's doing."

"My mom wants me to come to the 4-H building in an hour," Tony said, "so I'll bring Dolly back before that."

By the time Autumn had finishing braiding Beauty's mane and tail, a loudspeaker blared out the announcement that the cart competition would start in fifteen minutes.

Nathan felt the tension leave his body. With Autumn beside him, he didn't have anything to fear. "Help me hitch Beauty to the cart."

Not until they were seated in the refurbished cart with Dolly between them did Autumn realize how much like family they appeared. Dolly's animated gray eyes resembled Nathan's, and he must have thought the same thing. He grinned and shrugged his shoulders. Autumn supposed this would refuel the rumor that Dolly was their daughter. Perhaps when Trina took Dolly back to Wisconsin in a few days, the talk would die down.

"I hope you win, Mr. Holland," Dolly said.

"I'm not expecting to win. This is a tryout to prepare Beauty and me for future public appearances. Next year, I'll be serious about winning."

The past came back to Autumn as they circled the large field under the eyes of the judges, waving to the spectators crowding the fence and sitting in the bleachers. Summer stood beside the fence, and Dolly said, "There's Summer. Hi," she called, and Summer waved to them.

"Give me any advice you can," Nathan said, but he didn't need much coaching, for he had a masterful hand with the mare that reminded Autumn of her father. She was elated when Beauty came in second place to the Indian Creek Farm performance. It hurt a little that Jeff Smith drove the cart that won first place, especially since the cart was pulled by her own mare, Noel.

Forgive me my sins as I forgive those who sin against me, she prayed.

After Nathan stabled his mare, the three of them hurried to the bleachers to watch the Draft Horse Six-Hitch competition. Summer, dressed in a white party dress, sat beside her father when the shining black wagon pulled by six Weaver Belgians circled the ring. Moisture misted Autumn's eyes, and she could hardly see for a few moments. She blinked away the tears to watch as Landon exhibited all of the showmanship he'd learned through the years. Nathan reached for Autumn's hand and she clutched his fingers gratefully. He must realize how it hurt that she couldn't take her rightful place on the wagon with Summer.

"He hasn't lost his touch, has he?" Nathan said in admiration of the only man in the community who wouldn't speak to him.

Autumn nodded her head. Her throat was too tight for words when Landon pulled his six-hitch winners to a halt before the judges' stand and received the first place trophy. Summer's eyes searched the crowd until she saw her sister, and Autumn sensed the compassion Summer had for her.

Dolly took Nathan's hand when they left the bleachers, and he said, "Since you and Autumn helped me win a trophy, the least I can do is to buy your lunch. How about a hamburger and some fries?"

"I'm hungry," Dolly said, with a worried glance at Autumn's woebegone face.

"Sounds good to me, too," Autumn said, forcing a smile.

Putting aside her thoughts of the days when she'd reveled over Indian Creek Farm's achievements, Autumn enjoyed Nathan's company as he bought their lunch, which they sat on the ground to eat. Later, he went with them to the carnival and won a stuffed bear for Dolly at the shooting gallery.

"Thanks for being so good to Dolly, Nathan. She misses a father's influence. Her mother does well, but a child needs two parents."

"I haven't forgotten those few years after my father died," he said. "It's difficult growing up without a father."

Dolly ran ahead of them to stand in line by the

Ferris wheel, and he said quietly, "Have you ever thought that if we'd made different decisions years ago, we might have had a daughter like her?"

Autumn wouldn't meet his eyes. "More than once."

Squeezing her hand, he said, "Maybe it still isn't too late."

She glanced at him, wondering if he trusted her now, but she didn't get to find out, for Dolly was with them the rest of the afternoon. She didn't have a private moment with Nathan until she and Dolly left the fairgrounds, and he went to load his horse and equipment to return to the farm.

Hoping to sleep late the following Sunday morning, Autumn received a call about seven o'clock to care for a dalmatian that had been hit by a car. She was so despondent when she couldn't save the dog that she didn't go to Sunday school. She drove out into the country where she walked for an hour. Although Trina was a good encourager, when Autumn was depressed the need to be with her father was so keen that she nearly suffocated.

When she was a child, just a few minutes with Landon could calm all her fears and problems, so she wanted her Daddy now, but he didn't want her. Nathan would understand the pain she felt when she couldn't save an animal, couldn't give hope to a family who'd lost a beloved pet, but she wasn't going to bother him when he had a class to teach. She went home and dressed for worship, hoping she could spend the rest of the day with Nathan. Now that the fair competition was finished, she didn't know what excuse she'd have for going to Woodbeck Farm so often.

She entered the building just as Bible classes were dismissed, and she encountered Sandy and Ralph Simpson with Nathan in the foyer.

Sandy rushed to her and embraced her. "Our horse is doing great. We've brought him home, and the surgeon believes the horse will fully recover."

Autumn hadn't seen Ralph since she'd treated the racehorse, and he shook hands with her. "We owe you, Doc Weaver," he said, his broad face wreathed in a smile. "The surgeon told us that your treatment and decision to send the horse to him are what kept us from losing the animal."

"Thanks for telling me that. I wish all my cases could turn out so well," she answered.

Nathan must have detected her discouragement, for he drew her aside. "What's happened?"

"I had an early-morning surgery on a family pet dog that had been hit by a car. I did everything I could do, but it wasn't enough. I haven't been able to get the little girl's grief out of my mind."

Nathan laid his hand on her shoulder. "I'm sorry. Try to think of the many people you have helped, like the Simpsons," he said. "You're a good vet, Autumn, so don't doubt yourself."

Elwood's sermon text was "Forgiveness," and when he read the text, "Therefore, if you are offering your gift at the altar and there remember that your brother has something against you, leave your gift there in front of the altar. First go and be reconciled to your brother, then come and offer your gift."

While Elwood delivered his message, Autumn thought of the people she had wronged when she was a girl. Instead of getting mad at Nathan because he wasn't as fond of her as she was of him, she should have been sensitive to his struggle to make a place for himself on Indian Creek Farm to alleviate his poor economic situation. Under the circumstances, she felt she was justified in leaving Greensboro, but instead of running away without a word to her parents, she should have talked to them or at least have left a note explaining why she had to leave.

Dear God, she prayed as she contemplated the enormity of the pain she'd caused so many people, *what can I do to make restitution? All these years I've been dwelling on what my loved ones did to me and finding it hard to forgive them, and now I realize I was the worst offender.*

That afternoon, as Autumn returned from a call, she remembered another scripture from the Sermon on the Mount that Pastor Elwood had quoted in his message on forgiveness: "For if you forgive men when they sin against you, your heavenly Father will also forgive you. But if you do not forgive men their sins, your Father will not forgive your sins."

Autumn pulled the truck over to the side of the road, and bowed her head on the steering wheel. "God, I forgive them. I forgive Nathan for rejecting me. I forgive Mother for dominating my life. I forgive Daddy for not supporting me in my choice of a vocation. God, I brought most of these problems on myself. I forgive all of those who have trespassed against me."

The cleansing tears of repentance flooded her face and her spirit. A long time later, she lifted her head, wiped away the moisture from her face and anticipated the future with new determination. The misery was gone from her heart. Whatever happened she could make a life for herself. With or without Nathan and her family, she'd set her foot on the right path and she intended to continue that way. She would take the first steps of forgiveness and leave the results to God.

Chapter Sixteen

Intending to follow the direction the Holy Spirit was leading, Autumn telephoned Pastor Elwood on Monday morning.

"Pastor," she said, "your Sunday message spoke to me loud and clear. I've hurt a lot of people, and I want to make restitution. How much do you know about my past?"

"I don't listen to comments about a person unless they're positive, but my wife has heard that you left home several years ago and your family hadn't heard from you until you returned a few weeks ago. When a person wants to talk about her problems, I listen, but I don't like secondhand information."

Believing that her mother would be the worst hurdle in her path to forgiveness, Autumn said, "I need to seek reconciliation with my family. For years I've blamed them for how they'd wronged me, and they did to some extent, but I realize now it wasn't as bad as I imagined. I've achieved some rapport with my mother and sister since I've been here, and I want to start with them. But I'm too much of a coward to face them alone. Will you go with me to see them?''

"Certainly. When shall we go?"

"How about tomorrow morning at ten o'clock? Trina can handle the clinic by herself for a few hours, and my mother is more able to receive visitors in the morning. Her health is poor."

"I know. I've called at their home several times, but Mrs. Weaver wouldn't receive me. I'll be happy to go with you tomorrow. I'll stop by the clinic and pick you up."

Autumn knew it would be a long evening as she pondered how her mother would react to her visit. She wanted to talk to Nathan and get his prayer support. She tried to telephone him and was disappointed when he didn't answer. Leaving Trina and Dolly watching television with Miss Olive, Autumn put on tennis shoes and started out for a walk, wandering aimlessly down the street.

Walking head down, deep in thought, she'd gone several blocks when a red pickup drew up beside her.

"Lost?" Nathan said as he rolled down the truck's window.

"No. Moody! What are you doing in town?"

"Going shopping. Want to go along?"

"Might as well," she said, and walked to the right side of the pickup. He held the door open for her. As he started the car forward, she said, "Where are you going?"

"To the shopping center. There's a sale on light-bulbs. I must need to replace twenty or more. I've been too busy with haying and getting Beauty ready for competition to take care of little things. If I don't replace bulbs in the house and the farm buildings soon, I'll be wandering around in the dark.''

"How much of that big house do you use?"

"The kitchen, bedroom and bath. There are four big rooms upstairs, and four downstairs besides two large hallways. I probably haven't been upstairs for six months. It's too big a house for one person.''

"Your uncle lived there alone, didn't he?"

"Yes, after his mother died. I've always wondered what it would have been like to grow up on a farm like that, but my grandmother divorced her husband, moved away and had nothing more to do with the Hollands. Uncle Matt's mother was the second wife.''

"And he never married?" Autumn asked.

Nathan shook his head as he slowed down in traffic heading for the shopping district. "It's too bad he didn't marry and have a family to inherit his property, but if he had, I'd not be living there." He paused. "The past few weeks I've been thinking about myself. I'm almost thirty. If I want to have a family, I should marry soon, but I'm not sure I can afford to get married. How about you, Autumn? You ever thought about having children?"

She couldn't suppress a burst of laughter. If he was leading up to a proposal, he was certainly making a botch of it. At least his words had pulled her out of the doldrums.

When she laughed, he looked at her reproachfully.

"I was being serious!"

"I know, but your comments were ludicrous! No. I've given very little thought to having children. It's more satisfactory to have a husband, or at least the prospects of one, before contemplating a family.''

"Well, if you did have a husband or the prospects of one, would you want children?"

"Yes," she said simply. As he pulled into the parking lot of the shopping center, she dared to say, "But about being able to afford a wife, I've always heard that two can live as cheap as one."

"Do you believe that?"

"No," she said and laughed again. The trend of this conversation made her lighthearted. "But if you chose a wife who was earning a salary, your economic problem wouldn't be so serious."

"That's true," he agreed. "Something to think about."

Don't take forever, she thought. *Ray comes home soon.*

After Nathan bought the lightbulbs, they walked to a shop, ordered double-dipped cones of chocolate ice cream and sat on an outside bench to eat them.

"What made you moody?" he asked when they got in the truck and started toward the Wheeler residence.

"I'm going to see my mother tomorrow. I'm taking Pastor Elwood with me, and I hope to be reconciled with my mother. Sunday morning's sermon nudged me in that direction. Please pray for me, Nathan. I'm nervous about the way it will turn out."

"I'll do that. I believe when God prompts us to some action, the Holy Spirit goes with us, or before us, to intercede for us. You'll be all right. Let me know how it turns out," he said as he stopped in front of the Wheeler house. He leaned forward and kissed her.

"I'm pleased you asked me to go with you," she said. "I dreaded the long evening. Were you looking for me, by any chance?"

"Yeah. I drove by the clinic and Dolly told me you'd gone for a walk. Now that we don't have to work on the cart, are you going to stop coming to the farm?"

"Not if I'm invited."

"You have a standing invitation. Come when you want to. It's not very convenient for me to come to see you, with Trina, Dolly and Miss Olive present."

She held up her lips for another kiss and stepped out of the truck, more lighthearted than she'd been two hours ago.

Autumn telephoned the next morning and told Summer that she would be out for a visit. She didn't mention her purpose in coming.

"Daddy is in Columbus today," Summer said in a pleasant voice, "so this will be a good time for you to come. Mother's pretty good this morning."

It was a relief to know she wouldn't have to face both her mother and father the same day.

When the time neared for Pastor Elwood to arrive, with nervous fingers, Autumn took off the smock she'd been wearing in surgery and straightened the blouse and slacks she wore. As she applied a light coat of makeup and brushed her hair, Autumn said to Trina, "A lot hinges on this visit. Pray for me."

"I will. I've been praying for your reconciliation with the family for years because I could see how it was tearing you up inside. Every Christmas, when I'd go home to be with my family, I knew what a bleak holiday you spent."

"That wasn't your fault. You tried to get me to go with you." Taking Trina's hand, Autumn said, "Trina, I don't know how I ever found such a good friend as you've been to me. Have I ever told you how much I appreciate you?''

''Sure, lots of times, and that goes both ways,'' Trina answered with a broad smile that soon faded into a serious expression. ''But, remember, Autumn,'' Trina continued, and she gave Autumn a quick hug when Pastor Elwood drove into the clinic's parking lot, ''your mother may continue in her unforgiving ways, *but even if she does,* you've done your part. All you can do is sincerely ask to be forgiven, and if your parents won't forgive you, you can't make them. God can still give you peace of heart as long as you've been obedient to His commands.''

''I don't know how long we'll be gone,'' Autumn said as she opened the door.

''Don't worry about it. I'll take care of the clinic.''

Summer looked surprised when Autumn showed up at the door with Pastor Elwood, but she didn't refuse to let him enter. When Autumn started an introduction, Summer said, ''I know who he is.''

Elwood looked with interest at the spacious house with its antique furniture accumulated by several generations of Weavers as he followed Summer and Autumn down the hallway to Clara's bedroom. ''This is a beautiful house. Has your family always lived here?''

''It was built by our great-grandfather,'' Summer said, ''and our parents have lived here all of their married lives.''

''It's where my two sisters and I grew up,'' Autumn said.

''You must have had a pleasant childhood in such surroundings.''

"Yes. Yes, we did," Summer said, and her eyes met Autumn's, "but I didn't appreciate it as much as I should have."

"We were a close family when we were children, surrounded by the love of our parents. Sometimes, I'm sorry we had to grow into adults," Autumn added wryly, and Summer nodded in agreement.

Clara was plainly startled when they entered the room with the preacher.

"Mother," Autumn said, "I brought a friend with me. This is Elwood Donahue, the minister at the church Trina and I attend."

"I'd heard you'd turned religious."

Autumn winced at the sarcastic tone, but she was determined she wouldn't let her mother's attitude sidetrack her from her purpose.

"Good morning, Mr. Donahue," Clara continued, cordially enough. "Bring an extra chair, Summer."

Sunbeams filtered into the room through white miniblinds and lace curtains. A potpourri pot simmered on the dresser wafting an aroma of blooming lilacs around the room. Clara loved lilacs, and she'd planted a large grove of them near the white gazebo in the backyard. How thoughtful of Summer to provide her mother's favorite scent! Autumn looked at her sister with new appreciation. Even if Summer sometimes resented the role forced upon her, she was doing what she could to bring comfort to her mother. Summer had always been the most compassionate of the sisters.

When Elwood was seated in the platform rocker that Summer pushed close to Clara, Autumn sat on the floor beside her mother's chair. Praying for guidance in choosing the right words, she said, "Mother, it's true I have become religious, if you mean that I now have the desire for God and his Son, Jesus, to be the central focus of my life. For eighteen years, you and Daddy had been my focal point, had nurtured me and made my decisions. When I left home, I had nothing to cling to. I felt as lost as a sailor must feel when he's shipwrecked on an island. Everything that had sustained me was gone.''

Clara sat ramrod straight and lifted her hand. ''Autumn, I really don't want to hear this.''

''Mother, I *have* to get it off my mind and heart. Please listen.''

Clara lowered the forbidding hand and settled back in her chair.

''When I was separated from all of my loved ones, I remembered Bert and Spring, and what strength they had—how they'd given up everything to serve God. The time Spring came home from college and told us she'd become a Christian, I hardly knew what she meant, but I could tell she was different. Different from what she'd been before and certainly different from the rest of us. After leaving home, I felt so lost and desolate, and since I'd cut myself off from you and Daddy, I wanted the peace and comfort my sister had found. Trina's family showed me the way to find it.''

With her mother staring at Autumn with a stormy expression on her face, it was difficult for her to continue. She looked at Summer, who nodded encouragingly.

''My spiritual growth has been slow. It's hard for me to trust anybody, even God, to guide and provide for me. Yesterday, when Pastor Elwood preached a sermon on forgiveness, I realized what was standing in my way of becoming the confident, vibrant Christian I want to be.''

She paused, reached for Clara's hand and caressed it. Clara jerked her hand out of Autumn's grasp. Autumn couldn't remember that Clara had ever embraced her daughters or kissed them after they were old enough to start school, nor did she encourage her daughters to demonstrate affection toward her. She hadn't realized how much that had deprived her until she'd become acquainted with Trina's family, who were always hugging and kissing one another.

''I've come today to ask you to forgive me for the worry and pain I've caused you.''

''Get up off the floor and stop being so foolish!'' Clara said in a strong voice, almost as commanding as the tone she'd employed in disciplining her daughters. ''Weavers *do not* ask for forgiveness. We do what we think best and let the chips fall where they will.''

Autumn shook her head stubbornly. ''This Weaver needs to ask for forgiveness. I behaved very badly when I left Greensboro. My only excuse is that I hadn't matured much at eighteen, and I acted like a spoiled brat when I couldn't have what I wanted. I've wondered why I ever agreed to come back as Ray's helper when I had so many bad memories, but I believe now that God brought me back for a purpose. I can never become the person He wants me to be unless I make restitution for the past.''

Autumn turned toward her sister. ''And, Summer, I want you to forgive me, too. It wasn't fair for me to leave you with the responsibility you've had. Again, my only excuse is that I didn't know Mother was sick, but I could have found out. I've been selfish, and I want to make it up to you. Go back to school, pursue the career you've dreamed of. I'll set up practice somewhere in Ohio so I can check on Mother.'' She turned to Clara. ''Mother, it's time to let Summer go.''

''And it's time you tended to your own business,'' Clara said sharply. ''Summer recognizes her duty to her family even if you don't. If asking my forgiveness was the catharsis you needed to be relieved of past mistakes, then you've done what you came to do. You can leave now.''

Autumn's face blanched, and she felt Elwood's hand on her shoulder. Autumn stood on shaking legs that could scarcely hold her. Her throat was dry, but sweat drenched her body.

''I've not yet heard you say that you're sorry for disobeying your parents and going your own way. Apologizing for the way you carried on with Nathan Holland and shaming us before the whole community, would go a long way toward bringing you back into the family fold.''

Weaver pride asserted itself and Autumn answered, ''I won't apologize for something I didn't do. Nathan and I didn't 'carry on,' as you put it. He hadn't kissed me until that time Daddy found us in the barn. And come to think about it, I guess I'm not ready to receive forgiveness, either. I'm not sure I've forgiven the Weavers for how you treated Nathan nor for the way you've tried to ostracize him in the community since he's returned.'' She turned on her mother and motioned to Pastor Elwood.

Summer started to the door with them, and Clara said, ''Stay here, Summer.''

Summer defied her mother and put her arm around Autumn's waist as they left the house.

"I'm sorry, Autumn. She really misses you and wants you back, but she's too stubborn to admit it."

"Your support means a lot to me," Autumn said to her sister. She knelt to pet Spots, who lay on a blanket in a streak of sun. He wagged his tail. Counting Summer, that made two residents of Indian Creek Farm who still loved her.

"Uh-oh," Summer said, and Autumn looked up quickly. A blue minivan had driven into the parking lot and stopped beside Elwood's car.

"Daddy," Summer said quietly.

"I didn't think I could take on both of them today," Autumn said grimly, "but I guess I'll have to."

Autumn went down the steps and encountered her father as he rounded the side of his vehicle. "Hello, Daddy."

He halted his stride, looked quickly at her and tried to walk around her. "Please, Daddy," she said and took his arm.

He roughly pushed her hand off his arm. His gray eyes were cold and unrelenting. In the harsh and demanding voice she'd heard him use when he talked to his workers, but never to her, he said, "I am not your father. When you chose to leave this farm rather than to live as we wanted you to, you gave up any right to call it home. As far as I'm concerned, you are no longer a member of this family. Leave and never come back."

His words shook what little composure she had left, but she said, "Daddy, I've always loved you, and I always will. I'm sorry I've disappointed you, and also sorry that you no longer love me, but your feelings can't change how I feel about you or this farm. I might not be your daughter, but you're my beloved daddy and Indian Creek Farm will always be my home.''

She leaned forward and kissed his cheek. For a moment Landon's eyes connected with hers before he turned away and walked toward the barns with rigid back and deliberate stride.

The bravado Autumn exhibited while facing her father faded rapidly, and by the time Elwood had driven from the farmhouse to the highway, Autumn had slumped in the seat and buried her face in her hands.

Elwood laid a hand on her shoulder. "I'm sorry, Autumn, that was hard to take.''

She straightened in the seat and stared out the window, dry-eyed. "Pastor, I learned one important lesson today. Saying I'm sorry won't erase the mistakes of the past.''

"Saying I'm sorry is a good way to start reconciliation, but the words won't wipe out the disappointment, hurt and anger our actions have caused. The disciple Judas was sorry he'd betrayed Jesus, and he rejected the money he was paid for delivering Jesus to his enemies, but the deed was already done.''

"So what can I do?''

"Just what you're doing now. All anyone can do to promote reconciliation is to be truly sorry, ask for forgiveness and forgive in turn. Sometimes the offended parties will be of the same mind, but if they aren't, you've done all you can do.''

"Thanks for going with me today,'' Autumn said when Elwood stopped at Ray's clinic. "It was easier for me because you were there.''

Chapter Seventeen

The red roses arrived at the clinic soon after office hours started. Olive was in the office working on the monthly accounts, and she called, "Either of you girls expecting flowers?"

"Not me," Autumn called as she continued to groom the nervous white poodle.

"Tomorrow's the anniversary of when I got engaged," Trina said. "Maybe they're from my sweetie." She ran into the office, but returned in a few minutes, carrying a stemmed crystal vase holding a half-dozen red roses interspersed with greenery.

"Well!" Trina said. "They're for you!"

"From Mother?" Autumn asked, her spirits rising. Since Autumn's hands were busy, Trina removed the card and held it so Autumn could read the message.

Autumn said, "I can't take my eyes away from this dog. She's flighty today. You read it."

"'Congratulations on the fine vet you've become,'" Trina read. "'I'm happy you didn't let anything stop you from achieving that goal. How about a dinner date tomorrow night? I'll telephone in the morning. Nathan.'''

"Nathan!" Startled, Autumn gouged the palm of her hand with the clippers. "Ouch!" Her wound hurt, but she was glad she'd gotten the injury instead of the dog. She dabbed the puncture with a medicated swab, brushed the poodle, took it into the waiting room and delivered it to the owner.

Back in the exam room, she picked up the card and read it.

"Maybe he's suddenly afraid you might get away from him again," Trina suggested.

"But I can't go out tomorrow night. You're leaving in the morning."

"Sure you can. You didn't sell yourself body and soul to Ray Wheeler when you came here to work for him. Miss Olive will field the calls until you get back. When you start your own practice, you'll have to take some time off."

Smiling broadly, Autumn agreed. "This has been a long time coming."

Lighthearted over the pending date with Nathan, Autumn's thoughts turned to clothing. She'd saved most of the money she'd been paid as Ray's helper, so Autumn felt rich, but she still hadn't bought any dinner clothes. That afternoon she stopped in at a dress shop that sold medium-priced clothing and bought a light-blue classic sheath silk dress. Mrs. Varian, the saleswoman whom Autumn had known for years, raved about the effect Autumn's physique had on the dress.

"The dress looks as if it was made for you, so chic and charming. You have a model's body. Autumn, you could have had a great career in fashion, and you

chose to be a veterinarian.'' She spat the word out as
if it pained her and grimaced in disapproval.

The dress cost more than Autumn wanted to pay,
but it was the only one in the store that fit, and she
didn't have time to shop further. If the dress nurtured
Nathan's affection, it would be worth the price.

Trina's fiancé had spent the night in a local motel,
and by ten o'clock the next morning, Trina and Dolly
were on their way to Wisconsin. Trina had Autumn's
promise that she would be an attendant at her wedding
during the Christmas season.

Autumn had been busy in surgery since the clinic
opened, and she hardly had time to tell them goodbye.
Nathan was aware of their office hours, so he didn't
telephone until she closed the clinic at noon.

"Thanks for the roses," she said as soon as she
answered. "I've never had a bouquet of red roses before."

"What time shall I pick you up tonight?"

"I haven't said that I'll go with you."

"But you will, won't you?"

"I wouldn't miss it. Where are we going?"

"To a Middle Eastern restaurant in the Columbus
area. I sorta got hooked on Eastern food when I was
over there. You'll like this restaurant."

"I like anywhere I go with you. Even to an auction."

When they arrived at the restaurant, Autumn felt as
if she'd entered an Arabian Nights setting. The pungent odor of incense invaded her nostrils. Haunting,
discordant music greeted their entrance. Heavy drap-

eries covered the windows and hung from the ceiling. They walked on thick carpet.

Eyes gleaming in the faint light, Autumn said, "Have we entered the territory of Ali Baba and the Forty Thieves?"

He smiled and put his arm around her waist as they waited to be seated. She leaned against him.

"I like your new dress," he said.

"Bought especially for you," she said. "I've worn jeans for so long that I feel uncomfortable in a dress, but I wanted to please you."

"You have," he assured her.

He wore a brown suit, white shirt and tan tie, and Autumn thought he was the most handsome man in the room.

There were no individual tables. Patrons sat on cushioned benches at long tables along each side of the room. Dim light shone from wall sconces. Autumn didn't recognize most of the band instruments, nor did she understand a word of the singers' lyrics. The people sitting around them were strangers, but she and Nathan chatted with them when there was an interlude in the music.

The staff wore turbans, silk knee-length, sleeveless suits belted at the waist with wide girdles. They offered a choice of beverages, but otherwise, the meal was served family style. Autumn liked it. She was with Nathan. Everything was all right.

If they hadn't had a menu to guide them, Autumn wouldn't have recognized most of their food. When she commented on that fact, Nathan whispered in her ear, "Perhaps we'll enjoy the food more if we don't know what we're eating."

The appetizer was celery root with hazelnut sauce.

Next came a cup of plain yogurt with sliced cucumber seasoned with mint leaves and garlic, splashed with lemon. The salad was served with Turkish bread rings covered with sesame seeds. The main course was steak grilled over an open flame, spiced with a fragrant mixture of turmeric, caraway and cardamom, served with steamed rice and a variety of vegetables. The last course was a chilled Persian apple dessert made of raw apples and blended with lemon juice and orange flower water, accompanied by dark, strong coffee.

Symbolic of Middle East customs, the meal was served leisurely. Between courses, Autumn leaned against Nathan and his arms encircled her waist. The music was loud and conversation wasn't easy, but Autumn didn't care whether they talked or not. She thought how nice it would be to live in a fairy-tale world like this—just Nathan and her—and not have to return to the everyday world.

The floor show featured a dancer wearing a filmy white dress with a fancy girdle of gold around her waist. She wore a silk mask over the lower part of her face and swayed in rhythm to the music of a flute and a plucked instrument, which Nathan said was a *qanun*.

Despite the noise of the streets and the traffic on the interstate as they returned home, enjoyment of the evening lingered. Autumn tried to hum the music of the instruments but found that the melody didn't come easily to her lips.

"Thanks, Nathan. It's been a delightful evening. Too bad we have to return to work."

"I'd soon get bored with that kind of living, but I thought you'd like it for one evening."

"And I did. It was a change to have a real date, rather than to go do Jimmy's for a hot dog. Though I like that, too," she added hurriedly, for she knew he couldn't afford expensive evenings like this very often.

"Don't answer if it isn't of my business," he said, "but have you done a lot of dating?"

"I haven't dated anyone since I finished my first year of college. I was in a girl's school and learning how to date was part of our training. We were matched up with guys from a nearby college. Nathan, are you ever going to believe that I've never been interested in anyone else? I don't how I can convince you."

"I believe you, and I'll never ask you that question again. But I can't imagine why you haven't been pursued by lots of men."

"A woman can discourage a man easily enough when she isn't interested."

"I've gone out with several women, but only *once*. I guess no one could measure up to you."

"We've learned a lot about each other in these two months. That sudden separation eight years ago tore us apart before we got a chance to really know one another. If Daddy and Mother hadn't opposed us, we could have had a normal courtship."

"And saved a lot of heartache."

When they arrived at the clinic, Nathan walked with her to the front door of the darkened house. He kissed her and held her close. When he'd first met Autumn, her physical beauty had drawn him to her, but during these few weeks, he'd seen the *real* Autumn Weaver. He'd never known anyone with more compassion, tenderness, loyalty and love to offer. And he thought she was his for the asking. He was ready to speak the words that would bind them together, but was this the place to do it?

"Can you come to the farm tomorrow night? We need to have a long talk."

"I'll be there, Nathan. Thanks for a great evening." The words, *I love you,* hovered on her lips, but she suppressed them.

Thoughts of their pleasant evening together filled Autumn's mind as she worked in surgery the next morning, until near noon when Olive came into the room. She had a mysterious look on her face.

"Your father is on the phone, asking for 'Dr. Jackson.' His horses are sick. He sounds worried."

"You didn't tell him Trina is gone?"

Olive shook her head, and Autumn hesitated momentarily before she reached for the phone.

"Daddy, Trina has gone back to Wisconsin. I'll come out to see what's wrong with the horses."

"Don't bother," Landon said and hung up.

"I have a half notion to go anyway," Autumn said to Olive, and her blue eyes blazed in anger. "How dare he risk the health of his horses just because he's mad at me!"

"Give it some thought first," Olive advised. "Come in the house and eat your lunch before you make a decision."

"I've suddenly lost my appetite, but I'll try to eat."

"I've got spaghetti pie ready. You always like that."

"Do I have any calls for the afternoon?"

"Two or three, but nothing that can't wait if you decide to go to the farm."

"I'll be in soon."

After Olive left the clinic, Autumn leaned her head against the wall. *God, what can I do to mend the break*

*with my father? If I go to the farm now, it will only
make him more angry, but I can't let his stubbornness
endanger the health of the horses. How can a few
wrong decisions I made years ago have created such
a mess?*

Autumn scrubbed her hands and went into the
kitchen. She hadn't eaten more than a few mouthfuls
of the delicious spaghetti pie when her cell phone
rang. She took it from her pocket and answered.

"Autumn, this is Summer. I think you ought to
know that Noel is the horse that's in the worst condition. Daddy called for a veterinarian from Columbus,
but I went down to the barn and talked to Jeff Smith.
He's not sure the mare will live until that vet gets here.
I don't know anything about horses, but she's coughing and there's a heavy secretion from her nose."

"I'll be there immediately. Thanks, Summer."

Autumn explained the situation to Olive as she
grabbed a wedge of spaghetti pie and headed for the
door. "Will you cancel the other appointments? I'll let
you know what's going on as soon as possible."

Autumn was mindless of the speed limit as she
rushed out of Greensboro. The farm looked peaceful
when she parked beside the horse barn and hurried
inside to a stall where Landon and Jeff Smith stood
looking at Noel stretched out on the straw. When she
entered the stall, Landon gave an angry gesture, but
she brushed past him.

"Leave me alone, Daddy. I'm going to take care of
this horse. If you want the rest of your horses to die,
that's up to you, but Noel belongs to me."

She dropped to the floor beside the mare and
checked between the jaws and found that the lymph
glands were swollen. With a thermometer, she con-

firmed that the horse was running a high fever. When Jeff knelt beside her, she said, "This mare has the strangles," and he nodded.

"That's what I think, too."

Strangles was an infectious, transmissible disease, characterized by inflammation of the upper respiratory tract and by abscesses of the adjacent lymph nodes, that affected horses. Autumn broke out in a cold sweat, knowing that the infection could spread rapidly in the individual animal and to the rest of the herd. If not treated quickly and efficiently, the horse could die. In any event, it took a week or two for infected animals to fully recover.

Autumn looked up at her father, who stood in the doorway of the stall. She was surprised to see a look on his face that might have been tender, compassionate.

"How did this happen, Daddy? You've always been so careful before."

He turned and left without answering, and she looked questioningly at Jeff.

"Your father isn't as watchful of his workers as he used to be. The animals probably picked up this disease at the county fair. There might have been a contaminated hay rack or maybe the workers used a bucket or equipment from some other farm."

"Didn't he have them vaccinated?"

"I don't know."

Autumn put in a call to Olive. "Would you check Ray's records and see if he vaccinated Daddy's horses for strangles?"

Olive soon confirmed what Autumn suspected. The horses hadn't been vaccinated.

"Miss Olive, I'm going to stay here for a while, but

I'll send in for some supplies. If you're low on vaccine, have a shipment sent in immediately. Also, be sure we have plenty of antibiotics. You'd better alert the other horse owners in the neighborhood. Jeff thinks the horses might have been infected at the county fair, and if so, the disease could spread through the whole horse population of the county. As soon as I've done all I can here, I'll go to any other farm where I'm needed.''

"Are the other horses sick?"

"Not as bad as Noel, but they're coming down with it, too."

On her way to get some medication from the truck, Autumn passed by the office, and she paused momentarily. Her father sat at his desk, head bowed in his hands.

She wanted to go to him, put her arms around him and give him comfort. When anything was wrong with his horses, Landon was in pain, too. She knew she could help him more now by keeping his horses from dying than to comfort him, but her heart ached to see her once vibrant, energetic, father hunched over the desk like an old man.

"Poor Daddy!" she said to Jeff. "I don't know how he ever let this happen."

"You dad hasn't been himself the past few years. The burden of this farm is more than he can handle since Mrs. Weaver has been sick."

"Mother has been the dominant partner in the marriage, but he always took care of the mares. It used to be a neighborhood joke that Landon Weaver looked after his horses better than he did his family, which wasn't true. But I've never known Daddy to let his mares drink from a community watering tank, and he would never loan any equipment when he was away from the farm."

"He still wouldn't do it, but he's careless in supervising his hired hands, and they don't always do what he tells them to."

"No matter where the blame lies, the horses have strangles, and I have to do what I can to keep them alive."

"Although it's an infectious disease, it rarely results in death," Jeff said.

"That's true, but I don't want to have one of those rare occasions when I'm in charge. Will you send one of the workers into town to bring back the medications I asked Miss Olive to prepare? When that other vet gets here, Daddy will make me leave, but I'll do what I can in the meantime."

Jeff laughed lowly. "The other vet won't be coming. I heard Mr. Weaver telephone and cancel the order. I guess he realizes he has an expert medic in the family."

She flashed Jeff a smile of gratitude. "Then I pray I'll not disappoint him this time."

After checking the other stalls, where most of the mares showed signs of strangles, they went back to Noel. Violent coughing shook her whole body and her eyes were lackluster.

"All I can do now is administer antibiotics to prevent secondary infections and keep her warm. If you'll bring feed for her, I'll keep checking the other horses."

Autumn went from stall to stall, finding the eight animals in varied stages of sickness. One mare had no sign of strangles, and Autumn had a worker take the animal to a field and isolate her. Hopefully, the young stock out in the pasture could be kept from contacting the disease.

Straightening her back, after she'd taken the last mare's temperature, Autumn heard a sound behind her, and she turned quickly. Nathan had just entered the barn.

"Oh, Nathan," she said, hurrying to him. "Noel is sick."

"Yes, I know. Olive telephoned me about the emergency, and I came right away."

"Oh, I'm glad you did. Daddy doesn't want me to help, but I couldn't stay away and let the horses die. What if they die anyway? What if I don't know what to do?"

Nathan pulled her into his arms, and she nestled into his embrace. It felt good to surrender her weakness to his strength. He kissed her hair and massaged the muscles in her neck and shoulders.

"Don't think such things," he said softly. "You're a good vet, and you're more interested in the mares at Indian Creek Farm than any other person could be. Buck up. You've got a lot of hard work ahead of you."

"Will you stay with me?"

"As long as you need me. You know I'm not welcome at this farm either, but I won't leave until you do."

Reluctantly, she stepped out of his embrace. "Thanks, Nathan. How's your mare?"

"Okay for now. She's been vaccinated for the disease. What can I do to help?"

"I've sent into town for more antibiotics, and you can help me administer those when they get here. I want to put some hot packs on Noel's lymph nodes.

I'll probably have to incise and drain the abscesses, but hot packs will slow down the swelling. She won't like it, so you may have to help me restrain her.''

Nathan put his arm around Autumn's waist as they walked through the barn to Noel's stall. Landon stood in the office doorway, watching them, but he said nothing and neither did they.

Autumn was amazed when Summer showed up in the barn, for her sister had never liked the place. ''Is there anything I can do, Autumn?'' she asked, with a friendly nod in Nathan's direction.

''I need to put poultices on some of the mares, and it would be helpful if we had heating pads. Are there any at the house we can use?''

''I can find two or three. Anything else?''

''Maybe some heavy towels. We can soak them in hot water and put them on the mares' necks.''

''I'll be back soon.''

When Autumn checked Noel's fever again, it was higher than before. Worried, she placed a couple of the heating pads Summer had brought around Noel's neck, and Nathan helped her hold them in place. As they knelt side by side on the straw floor, their eyes met and their gazes locked.

''Kinda like old times, huh?'' Nathan said.

''I was thinking the same thing. This is the stall where Noel was born, where we met for the first time. What a lot of things have happened since then.''

''I did a lot of thinking about us last night, remembering the words of the Apostle Paul, 'Forgetting what is behind and straining toward what is ahead, I press on...' Autumn, you weren't the only one who made mistakes in the past. I made some, too, and I wonder if God has given me another chance, and I'm too stupid to take advantage of it.''

''Oh, Nathan,'' she whispered. He learned forward and brushed his lips against hers, but they straightened when they heard approaching footsteps. Jeff came into the stall with a bag of supplies.

''Miss Olive,'' he reported, ''says two of the Simpson horses are sick, and there are two other farmers who want you to vaccinate their stock. She's ordered vaccine, and it will be in on the morning delivery truck.''

Autumn left Nathan to watch over Noel, and Jeff helped her medicate the other animals, none of which were as sick as Noel. It had been dark for hours when she got back to Noel's stall, where Nathan reported, ''I think she's better. Her wheezing isn't as noticeable, and she doesn't cough as much.''

Autumn patted the Belgian's head and ran her hands over the sleek hide. ''Oh, I'm so thankful.'' When she checked Noel's temperature, it had dropped three degrees. Autumn swiped the tears from her eyes. She had no time for weeping.

''Jeff,'' Autumn said to the trainer, ''I'm responsible for taking care of all of Ray's customers, so I'll have to leave. Can you take care of things now? If not, maybe Nathan can stay for a few hours.''

Autumn wasn't aware that Landon had been watching from the stall door until he spoke. ''You've done the hard work, and there's no reason I can't take over now,'' he said in tones that were reminiscent of the Landon of her youth. ''If I need help, Jeff will be here. You need to rest.''

''No rest for me tonight because I've got several other calls to make. We need to stop this disease before it spreads farther. I do believe everything is all right here, but I'll stop by again in the morning." She turned to Jeff. "In the meantime, I'll keep my phone with me, and if Noel takes a turn for the worse, you get in touch with me." She smiled at her father. "I had too much trouble bringing Noel into the world to lose her now."

He didn't return her smile, but he looked at his watch and said gruffly, "You and Nathan haven't had anything to eat or drink for hours. There's some food at the house."

"Thanks, Daddy, but I'll grab a bite in town. I have to go back to the clinic for vaccine, and Miss Olive will probably have more calls for me now." She reached a hand to Nathan. "Thanks, Nathan, for helping."

He took her hand and, in spite of the watchful eyes of Landon, drew her into a cozy embrace. "I'm going with you. I probably won't be much help with the animals, but I can drive while you catch a few winks of sleep between farms. I won't let you spend this night on the roads alone."

His words didn't provide any room for disagreement, and besides, she wanted him with her.

"Let's go."

"I'll get my truck when we stop by here tomorrow," Nathan said. They took off their contaminated coveralls and washed at the laundry near the office.

"There are clean boots in the truck," Autumn said. "I think you can wear Ray's boots. We'll have to be careful not to carry the disease with us."

She handed Nathan the keys, and she climbed into the passenger's seat. Landon stood in the doorway and watched them leave, but he didn't respond when Autumn waved. Sighing deeply, she leaned her head against the leather upholstery.

"Did you notice we received a rather left-handed invitation to go to the house?" Nathan asked, amusement lighting his gray eyes.

Grinning at him, she said, "I noticed, and I wish we could have gone, but I don't have any time to waste. It would have taken longer than to stop for a couple of hamburgers."

"I believe your father's anger is slowly fading. He couldn't help but be impressed with the way you handled your job tonight. Perhaps he's realizing he may have made a few mistakes in the past, too."

"I hope so. I love my daddy so much, and it's frustrating not to have him to lean on."

Chapter Eighteen

Autumn dialed the clinic's number and when Olive answered, she said, "Everything is under control at Indian Creek Farm, Miss Olive, and I'm heading back to town. Nathan is with me. We'll be there as soon as we stop for something to eat."

"Don't dare stop at a restaurant. I have a meal waiting for you," Olive said sternly. "There's plenty for Nathan, too. I'll have the food on the table, and while you eat, I'll put all the provisions you need in the truck. Eating a decent meal won't delay you at all. I don't know why veterinarians think they can go day and night without food and rest," she grumbled as she hung up the phone. Autumn knew the remark was aimed at the absent Doc Wheeler as much as at her.

The aroma of freshly prepared food assailed their nostrils when they walked into the kitchen. Olive had two plates filled with chicken and noodles and fresh green peas, and a bowl of vegetable salad already on the table. She placed a pan of hot biscuits between them and poured tall glasses of iced tea.

Autumn grabbed the glass of tea and drained it before Nathan had time to say the blessing. "Oh, Miss Olive, thank you. I didn't realize how thirsty I was until I saw the glass."

"Now you just sit down and eat." Olive clucked like a mother hen as she rustled around the kitchen. "And I've got beef sandwiches in a cooler for you to take with you, as well as a large thermos of coffee. You're going to have a long night."

When Nathan and Autumn expressed their thanks as they left the clinic, Olive said, "I've looked after one vet for twenty-five years, so I've learned a few things." She stood by the truck as they prepared to leave the driveway and looked in the open window. With a gentle smile, she said, "It's good to see the two of you together."

They went first to the Simpson farm where two horses were sick. Ralph had already isolated the infected animals from the rest of his herd, and after Autumn gave the animals antibiotics to prevent secondary illness, she gave Ralph instructions on what to do.

The next farmer had a riding horse for his children. The abscess on the horse's lymph nodes had matured to the place where she had to incise and drain the swelling, but she thought antibiotics would take care of the situation.

They visited three more farms without any problems, but Autumn administered vaccine in an effort to prevent the spread of the disease. By the time she'd made the last call Olive had put on her work order, daylight had come and Autumn could barely walk to the truck. Nathan lifted her bodily and placed her in the seat. He had been her tower of strength all night long, but she was too weary to tell him so.

"I'm going to take you back to Greensboro and tell Olive to put you to bed."

She shook her head. "Not yet. Let's go by Indian Creek Farm. I can't rest until I know that everything is under control there."

While Nathan drove the few miles to the farm, Autumn dialed the clinic. "Anything new?" she asked.

"No more emergencies," Olive said, "and I've canceled the surgery appointments for this morning. You come home and go to bed," she ordered.

"I'll be there soon," Autumn promised.

Sleepy-eyed, Landon met them at the door of the barn, and Autumn knew he hadn't slept, either.

"Noel is out of danger, I'm sure," he said as if he knew that was most important to her.

"Great," Autumn said, stifling a yawn. "I can sleep now, but I'll take a quick look around. I'm still responsible to Ray, and he'll want a report."

Noel was on her feet, still wheezing and coughing occasionally, but she nibbled at the oats in her feed box. Autumn leaned against the mare for a few moments before she checked the abscess. Looking at Landon, she said, "I'd better incise and drain it, shouldn't I?"

"I think so, but you're the doctor."

"Nathan, if I can impose on you a little longer, please bring the instrument case in, and I'll take care of it." She patted the mare's neck. "This will hurt a little, Noel, but it will make you feel better."

The other mares were either stable or improving, so Autumn felt free to leave them after she'd drained the abscess. Her father was as knowledgeable about Belgians as any veterinarian, and now that he seemed to be his old self, he could handle the mares.

Nathan handed her the keys to Ray's truck. "Are you sure you can stay awake? I can take you home."

"No, I'm fine. Thanks for going with me tonight."

"I'm following you into Greensboro to be sure you get back safely. If you get sleepy, pull over."

It was comforting to have his red pickup trailing her into town. After being on her own for eight years, making her own decisions and taking care of her personal problems, it seemed like paradise to have someone watching over her. When she drove into the clinic's parking lot, Nathan tooted his horn and went on by.

Autumn fell across her bed without even undressing, and it seemed like no time before she felt a gentle touch on her shoulder. Olive stood beside the bed with a tray holding a pot of tea and two cinnamon rolls. She placed the tray on a small table and drew it close to the bed. She handed Autumn a warm, damp washcloth.

Autumn yawned, stretched and listened to the clock striking in the hallway.

"Two o'clock," she said. "I didn't intend to sleep so long. Why didn't you waken me?"

"Sit up," Olive said "and take a little nourishment."

The warm cloth felt so good on her dry face, which Autumn also discovered had been a dirty face when she looked at Olive's white washcloth.

"I'd better take a shower before I eat," she said.

Olive fluffed several pillows behind Autumn's back and placed the tray in front of her. "Eat first."

Obediently, Autumn ate the warm pastry and sipped on the tea, while Olive straightened the room. "I washed your clothes yesterday," she said, "so you have plenty of fresh shirts and jeans in the closet."

"Thanks, Miss Olive. With Nathan watching over me day and night, and you pampering me, it's going to be hard to go back to taking care of myself."

"You need a little pampering now."

Autumn finished the last of the tea and handed the tray to Olive. "Thanks. That was good, as were those sandwiches you made for us last night."

"I don't believe in giving bad news on an empty stomach, and I've got bad news."

Autumn's lethargy was forgotten, and she stiffened. "Noel? Did Noel die?"

"As far as I know, everything's all right at Indian Creek Farm. Nathan's filly is sick now."

Autumn swung out of bed, her feet hitting the floor with a thud. "Why didn't you call me before?"

"Nathan telephoned a couple of hours ago, but he made me promise not to tell you until you awakened. I broke that promise, because I knew you'd never get over it if you slept on when he needed you."

Autumn rushed down the hall to the bathroom and took a quick shower. Back in her room, she put on the clothes that Olive had placed on the bed. In the clinic, Olive held out a pair of clean coveralls and the boots Autumn had worn yesterday, now scrubbed and disinfected.

"I'm getting far behind with the clinic calls. Maybe you should call in a vet from another county. I'm going to stay with Nathan as long as he needs me."

"We don't have anything yet that can't be put off. If an emergency arises, I'll decide then. Go on, and don't worry about things here at the office."

* * *

Nathan hurried from the barn when she drove into the barnyard. His face was gaunt with worry.

"I don't know what happened," he said. "Beauty had been in the barn all day yesterday, and I checked on her when I came in this morning. I thought she was all right. I went into the house and slept for a couple of hours, and when I came back to the barn, she was sick."

"How sick?"

"*Real* sick."

Autumn heard the filly coughing before she got into the barn, and she followed the sounds to the stall. Nathan had already applied hot packs to the rapidly swelling lymph nodes, and when Autumn checked, she found the horse's temperature extremely high.

"I brought antibiotics. Maybe they'll help. You did say she'd been vaccinated?"

"Yes. Ray did that when he gave her the other shots she needed, but I've heard there are cases where a horse doesn't build an effective immune system even if it is vaccinated."

"Do you know how she became infected?"

He shook his head. "I've been careful. It's possible someone may have borrowed a pail or a bridle at the fair when I wasn't looking and the disease was transmitted that way."

"Nathan, I feel so inexperienced. I've seen cases of strangles in vet school and studied about the infection, but this is the first time I've treated horses for the disease. Maybe I'm doing everything wrong. Can we take her to Columbus? Or perhaps call another vet? If Ray only was here, he'd know what else to do."

Nathan realized that Autumn was at the breaking point, and he took her hands. "Look at me, Autumn."

When her eyes met his, he said, "Believe me, there's no vet on earth I'd trust any more than I do you. You can do as much as another vet. I trust you implicitly."

"But what if she dies?"

"I won't blame you. Do what you think is necessary."

After she administered the antibiotics, they applied hot packs, and kept the animal as comfortable as possible. For the next three days, Autumn and Nathan kept watch over Beauty around the clock. While one of them watched, the other stretched out on a pile of hay in the barn. Ralph Simpson came with sandwiches and hot coffee. They ate, not because they were hungry, but because they needed the strength the food would generate. Jeff drove over from Indian Creek Farm and added his expert advice. There was a constant stream of visitors from worried neighbors, reporting that Autumn's treatment had apparently stopped the spread of the infectious disease.

The filly's fever continued to rise. Autumn would no sooner incise and drain one abscess, than another would form, and Beauty struggled to breathe when the swelling in her throat increased. Nothing seemed to help.

As the horse slowly died, Autumn wondered why, of all the other animals she'd worked with over the past four days, that it was Nathan's only Belgian that had to die. When the mare breathed her last, Autumn leaned her head on the dead animal and sobbed.

His own eyes full of tears, Nathan pulled Autumn upward and guided her out of the stall to the feed room, where he sat on a bale of hay and drew her down beside him.

"It's all right, Autumn. It's all right. You can't save all of your patients."

"But why did it have to be yours, Nathan? I'd rather have lost Noel than for your Beauty to die. Of all the animals I've worked with, why did yours have to die?"

"I don't know the answer to that, sweetheart, but you did all that was possible. Go back to the clinic, and get it off your mind. I'll take care of things here."

"I'm so sorry, Nathan." She put her arms around him and lifted her lips for a kiss. Nathan wasn't slow to respond, and his tender passionate caress brought more relief to her spirit than anything else could have done. They were closer than they'd ever been.

"Promise me something," he whispered with his face buried deep in her disheveled chestnut hair. "Don't leave Greensboro right away. Stay for a while, even after Ray comes home."

She nodded. "I promise."

Autumn was relieved he'd extracted the promise from her, for when she arrived at the clinic, sturdy, broad-shouldered Ray Wheeler came out to greet her. In spite of her fatigue, she jumped out of the car and ran to him. He whooped and pulled her into a tight embrace.

"How's my new vet?" he asked.

"I've never been so glad to see anyone in my life," she shouted, but then she pulled out of his arms and pommeled his broad chest with her fists. "How dare you talk me into coming here? What I've gone through the past two months is enough to make me wonder why I ever wanted to be a vet! You scoundrel," she added.

Laughing loudly, Ray grabbed her hands. "Stop it!

I did you a favor, and you know it. Olive tells me you've had a rough week.''

"Well, yes, you could say that. And last night was the worst of all. In spite of all I could do, Nathan's horse died.''

"I'm sorry, but you had to learn sooner or later the worst nightmare of our profession. We're not God, and we can't perform miracles.''

"I know that, and I'd have been sad to have had any animal die, but it hurt especially bad when it was Nathan's only horse.''

"Come in for breakfast, and then you'd better get some rest. I can take over now.''

They walked into the house and sat down for a meal of pancakes and sausage. Miss Olive's face shone as she waited on them. Her beloved brother was home at last!

"When did you get home?''

"A half hour ago. I was getting ready to come to Woodbeck Farm to see if I could help when you drove in.''

"But don't you have jet lag? You'll need to rest, too.''

"No. The plane got into Chicago too late to make connections, so I rented a car and started driving. When I got to Indianapolis, I could hardly stay awake, so I took a motel room, slept several hours, and then drove on. I feel fine now.''

"I'll take a nap and start working on the backlog of calls that have accumulated. Will you go check all the horses that have strangles? I'd intended to do that this morning, but I'd rather you did it.''

"I'll take care of it.'' He finished the last of his pancakes and settled back in his chair. "Now, let's discuss something very important for both of us. I want you to stay on with me, Autumn, not just as my assistant, but as a full partner in the business.''

''I appreciate that, Ray, but I can't give you my decision now. I will, however, stay at least a month to help you get caught up. This past week when I've been busy with the horses, Miss Olive has had to postpone all the regular appointments. You'll need some help.''

''I've learned a lot from the other veterinarians while we've been traveling, and I'd like to expand into new areas of services. I can't do that without help.''

''I'll give you an answer within a month. It's too weighty a decision for me to make right now.''

''Thanks for taking over for me, Autumn.''

''A more experienced person could have done better.''

He shook his head in disagreement. ''I doubt it, especially with the strangles. You've learned the latest techniques. You love horses, and you've always had unusual canny when it came to dealing with them. I suppose you inherited that from Landon. And by the way, have you patched things up with your family?''

''I've visited with Mother and Summer a few times. Not with Daddy. He wasn't going to let me treat his Belgians, but I forced my way past him and took over. Short of carrying me off the farm, he couldn't get rid of me, and he did mellow a little before the night was over. Nathan came to help, and Daddy actually invited us to go to the house and have something to eat.''

''Landon will come around. You'll see.''

''I hope so. That's one of the reasons I've agreed to stay a few more weeks. If you'd asked me to stay a week ago, I'd have refused.''

''What's the other reason you've agreed to stay?''

"You ask too many questions," Autumn retorted. "Thanks for the breakfast, Miss Olive. I'm going to shower and take a nap. Please don't let me sleep past noon."

Nathan had held up a brave front before Autumn because he didn't want her to feel any more downcast than she already did over the death of Beauty, but it was one of the hardest blows he'd experienced. Since the first day he'd gone to Indian Creek Farm and saw the Weavers' herd of Belgians, he'd set his goal to one day own a herd of his own. He'd thought Beauty was the beginning of his dream, but now he was back where he started. The money he'd borrowed to buy the filly, to renovate the farm buildings and improve the land had been a large debt that would take several years to pay. The horse was insured, but not to the extent he could buy another filly now.

His dream of owning Belgians had been dashed to the ground, but his dream of having Autumn had been revived. During the night when he realized the filly was dying, he made up his mind that this time Autumn wouldn't get away from him. When his heart was so heavy with the loss of Beauty, he couldn't speak to her, but he had her promise. He'd soon make up for the way he'd treated her. He should have known she was sincere when she'd told him how much she cared for him. If he'd ever doubted it, he no longer did. A devotion that could survive eight years of separation had to be fed by a strong love.

Ralph came with a back loader to help Nathan dispose of the filly's carcass. While Ralph dug a large hole near a wooded area west of the creek, Jeff arrived with a hoist from Indian Creek Farm, and he helped

Nathan lift the filly's body and take it to the grave. Nathan turned his back when Ralph started covering the Belgian's body with dirt.

With a grateful wave to Jeff and Ralph, he started his tractor and drove to a field beyond the house where he spent the rest of the day preparing the soil for a winter crop of wheat. When he returned late in the evening, he avoided the pasture where he'd kept Beauty. He'd always thought of Autumn when he worked with the Belgian, and there had never been a day when he hadn't spent some time with the animal. The hurt was too much to bear today.

Physically and mentally fatigued, Nathan went to bed early, but his sleep was troubled. He dreamed of Beauty, and he dreamed of Autumn. Morning found him sluggish and grouchy. Ray Wheeler was his first visitor.

Ray shook hands with Nathan. "I stopped by to see you yesterday, but you weren't at home. I'm sorry about your loss. I wish I could have been home, but it wouldn't have been any different if I'd been here."

"No. Autumn is a good vet."

"I'm finding that out," Ray said. "Yesterday, I went to all the horse farms, and she treated the animals exactly as I would have done. A lot more horses might have died if she hadn't known what she was doing and kept the disease from spreading. I'm trying to get her to stay on."

Nathan looked away and didn't comment.

"She told me yesterday she'd stay for another month, but I'm hoping to make it permanent. I want to expand my business, and with the high praise all these farmers have for her now, she won't have to be concerned about her standing in the community. I understand from Olive that she hasn't been accepted very well by some of her former neighbors, but after I put in a few good words about her abilities, she'll be looked up to as she used to be. 'The Weaver tomboy who knows as much about horses as her father does.'"

Nathan's eyes filled with mirth. "If that little speech was designed to convince me, you wasted your time, Doc. I've been sold on Autumn Weaver for a long time."

"Then why don't you do something about it, man?"

"I'm working on it. Give me time!"

"Time! You've had eight years."

"Yeah. Eight years when I didn't even know where she was! If she stays in Greensboro for a month that should be all the time I need," he stated. Then he added pointedly, "That is, if everybody else will back off and let us handle it ourselves."

"Touché," Ray said. "I'll say no more."

Chapter Nineteen

With Ray taking care of the farm calls, Autumn spent a busy day in the clinic. She was ready to close, when she received a telephone call from Summer.

"All seems to be well with the horses," she reported. "Daddy says that none of them is any worse, and he believes they're starting to improve."

"Did you hear that Nathan's horse died?"

"Yes. I'm sorry about it, Autumn, and believe it or not, so are Mother and Daddy."

"It wouldn't have been so bad if it wasn't the only Belgian he owned."

"I called about something else that I think will make you feel better. Mother wants you to come to see her and bring Pastor Elwood with you."

"Well! That is a surprise."

"She suggested tonight."

"Will Daddy be there?"

"I don't know. He's spending most of his time in the barns right now."

"If Pastor Elwood is free, we'll come out in a few hours."

Two hours later, with a great deal of trepidation, Autumn parked in front of the old Victorian home. Pastor Elwood sat beside her.

She sighed. "I'm almost afraid to go in. So much hinges on this visit," she said.

"Your mother wasn't far from reconciliation when we were here before. She's a proud woman, and it's hard for her to change her mind."

Summer met them at the door.

"Daddy isn't here. He had a trip into Greensboro. I don't think he knew you were coming."

Clara waited for them in the living room, and when Autumn bent to kiss her cheek, Clara didn't rebuff her.

"Sit down, Pastor Elwood. Autumn," Clara said. Going immediately to the reason for the visit, she continued, "I want you to know that I'm proud of you and your skill as a veterinarian. Landon praises you highly for the work you've done in the community these past few days. You came to apologize to me once and I wouldn't accept the apology."

Autumn knelt beside her mother's chair and took her hand.

"It's I who must apologize. I was wrong. You were right in your desire to become a veterinarian. I shouldn't have insisted that you do what I wanted. I'm sorry, but I want you to know, I was doing what I thought was best for you."

Tears softened Autumn's eyes. "I know, Mother. I never doubted that."

"It's not easy to say I'm wrong, knowing that my actions almost ruined my daughter's life."

Clara's face flushed. Tears formed in her eyes and rolled down her cheeks. If Clara had ever cried before, Autumn had never witnessed it.

Autumn perched on the side of Clara's chair and drew her mother into a close embrace. "Mother," Autumn said, "I love you, and I appreciate all the things you've done for me. What I considered dominance was your way of guiding me, and I would have been better off if I hadn't been so rebellious. We can't do anything about the past, but the future is before us. Are you willing to make a fresh start?"

Clara's head dropped to Autumn's shoulder and she nodded emphatically. "God bless you, Mother. You've taken a load off my conscience."

Autumn felt an arm around her waist, and she turned to see Summer kneeling beside them with the other arm around her mother.

"I need to ask for your forgiveness, too," Summer said. "I've been resentful of you and Spring, of the fact that I had to stay at home. And it isn't all Mother's fault, either. She didn't demand that I come home. I felt compelled to do so, and I'm happy I could take care of her."

Clara lifted her head and caressed Summer's cheek. "But Autumn is right, Summer. I want you to go on with your education. I shouldn't have accepted your sacrifice, but I, too, felt alone. I could hardly bear to think of all my daughters leaving me. My whole life had been wrapped up in you, and I had nothing left when one by one you began leaving home. I do appreciate the years you've devoted to me, but I'm setting you free now. It's not too late to get the education you want and pursue a career of your liking."

"Thank you. I'll be thinking about it."

Turning again to Autumn, Clara said, "After you came home and I heard how efficiently you were taking over Ray's work, I've wished more than once that I'd allowed you to follow your dream of becoming a vet. You've achieved your goal, but you did it without us. We could have made it so much easier for you, but we missed eight years of your life."

"I've never regretted the hard work it took to get through vet school. I'd had too much given to me. It changed my whole perspective on life when I had to work. And I doubt very much that I would ever have accepted Christ into my life if I hadn't depended upon my faith in God to see me through. As rich Autumn Weaver, I didn't have time for God. When I was separated from my family, I drew closer to Him. The hope of eternal security I have now is worth the trials of the past years."

Elwood had remained silent during this exchange, and until he spoke, Autumn had actually forgotten his presence in the room.

"Ladies," he said, "shall we have prayer? This has been a beautiful demonstration of what can result when we're obedient to the spirit of God. Because Autumn obeyed God's command and asked to be forgiven, all of you have found happiness."

"I still have a long way to go," Autumn said, "but after today, the rest of my goal to set things right will be easier."

After Elwood prayed, Clara dispatched Summer to the kitchen to speak to Mrs. Hayes about some refreshment for their guests. Elwood asked permission to look around the farm and Autumn and her mother were left alone.

"Autumn," Clara said, "I won't interfere with your

decisions again, but I would like to know what your plans are. Also, I've heard gossip about that child you brought with you. Will you clear that up?''

''Dolly is exactly the way we've presented her. Trina's sister is a single mother, and the woman who usually sits with Dolly during summer vacation became ill suddenly and had to have surgery. We volunteered to care for Dolly until her sitter was recovered or until school started. Her sitter is better now, and Trina took Dolly home last week. I'll admit the child does look like Nathan, but he doesn't even know Dolly's mother. And, Mother, please believe me when I tell you that nothing happened between Nathan and me that could have produced a child. Furthermore, I haven't been involved in sexual immorality with anyone.''

Clara lifted her head, shocked, and Autumn expected a reprimand for discussing such a subject openly. Clara paused briefly before she said, ''I'm glad to hear it. All of my teachings weren't wasted.''

''None of your teachings were wasted, I assure you.''

''You have no interest in Dr. Lowe?''

Autumn shook her head. ''None at all. He's a fine man, but not the person I want for a mate. I'm sure he feels the same about me.''

''What do you intend to do?''

''I'll stay for another month to help Ray catch up on the work. He's offered me a job leading to a full partnership eventually, which would be fine, for I could be here to look in on you.''

''Are you going to accept his offer?''

''I don't know. That depends.''

''Depends on what?'' Clara demanded.

"A couple of things, but one of them is Daddy's forgiveness. I can't be much help to you when I have to sneak in and out of the house when he's gone."

Clara waved her hand. "Landon is full of pride and bluster. I'll bring him around. In spite of his worry over the horses, he's been happier the past twenty-four hours than he's been for years. That's because you're home." She looked sternly in Autumn's direction, but the autocratic, domineering attitude was gone. "What about Nathan Holland?"

"What about him?" Autumn said, suppressing a smile.

"Are you going to marry him?"

"That's up to Nathan. My love for him is stronger than it was when I was a girl, but he's hesitant to make a commitment. Losing that expensive filly won't help matters."

"I was wrong about him, too. I understand he's become a good farmer. I have no objection to him now, but I still believe if you'd run away with him years ago, you would both have been miserable."

"You're probably right, but the way things turn out between us will determine whether I stay at Greensboro. I would enjoy working at Ray's clinic, but not if Nathan keeps his distance. I promise you, though, I won't go so far from home that I can't keep in touch with you."

Summer came in carrying a tray and Elwood followed her. Summer passed around cups of coffee and a plate of cookies.

"I see Mrs. Hayes hasn't lost her skill at baking peanut butter cookies. They were always my favorite," Autumn said as she bit into the rich pastry.

They spent a pleasant half hour, and Autumn kept

hoping her father would come home. She would have liked to be reconciled to him before she saw Nathan again.

When Elwood and Autumn made preparations to leave, Autumn leaned over and kissed her mother's forehead.

"Autumn," Clara said, unable to resist advising her youngest daughter, "you're working too hard, and it shows in your looks. You need to gain some weight. Once your beauty is gone, you've lost everything."

Laughing, Autumn said, "I haven't lost anything, and I've gained a lot tonight. Reconciliation is a beautiful thing."

Summer placed her arm around Autumn's waist when they reached the back porch. "Thanks, Autumn. I hope things go well between you and Nathan."

"Me, too."

"And don't worry about Daddy. He'll make up with you."

As soon as Autumn returned to town, she put in a call to Nathan.

"I've got wonderful news," she said as soon as he answered the telephone, and she gave him a detailed version of the visit to her mother. "I wish Daddy could have been there."

"That's wonderful, my dear. And don't worry about your dad. He's already mellowing toward you. I'd hoped you'd come here tonight, but it was more important to see your mother."

"I'll come to see you tomorrow."

Nathan spent the next morning cleaning out the stall where Beauty had died and disposing of the refuse. He disinfected the stall and everything the horse could have contacted. He put away her halter in the tack room with the cart and harness, wondering if he'd ever need the equipment again. He'd just finished the distasteful task when the Indian Creek Farm truck and stock trailer pulled in and stopped beside the barn. Jeff Smith was driving, with Landon Weaver sitting in the passenger's seat. This was his first visit to Woodbeck Farm since Nathan had moved in.

Jeff stepped briskly out of the truck, calling, "Hi, Nathan. Brought you something." He walked to the rear of the trailer. Landon opened the truck door, swung his feet out on the running board and continued to sit in the truck for a few minutes surveying the farm buildings.

"You've made a lot of improvements here. The place looks better than it has for years."

"Yes, sir, but I still have a long way to go before Woodbeck Farm looks like it did when I used to visit here as a boy. Uncle Matt had let the place run down before he died."

Landon stepped to the ground. "As we get older, we have a tendency to let important things slide. I'm ashamed that Indian Creek Farm doesn't look the way it once did, but I've learned my lesson. There'll be some changes made."

There wasn't much Nathan could say to this comment. His attention drifted to the horse trailer where Jeff had disappeared, wondering what the trainer was doing.

"We heard about your horse dying, Nathan, and I'm sorry," Landon said. "If you hadn't come to help Autumn, the same thing might have happened at our farm."

"Your horses okay now?"

"Doing well, Doc Wheeler says. I'm thankful that my carelessness didn't cause a catastrophe. I've been doing a lot of soul-searching the past twenty-four hours. Clara and I want to replace what you've lost." He turned around and said, "Bring her out, Jeff."

Jeff led a young Belgian filly around the side of the trailer. The animal was skittish of new surroundings and she struggled against the halter rope. Her sleek coat gleamed like burnished gold in the midday sun, and the strip down her face was snow-white. Nathan stared at the filly, and her intelligent eyes seemed to survey him as she walked close to him, bared her teeth and gingerly nibbled his shoulder. Nathan put his arm around her neck and she didn't budge. It was a case of mutual love at first sight.

"This is Cupid," Landon said. "Noel's foal born on Valentine's Day. She's yours, Nathan."

"Oh, no, sir," Nathan stammered. "I can't afford a filly like this."

"There's no price tag attached, son. She's yours."

"No, sir, I won't accept it. Thanks anyway." Although his lips refused, Nathan still kept his arm around the Belgian as she nestled against him.

Landon stepped close to Nathan and laid a hand on his shoulder.

"Take the filly and make two overly proud people happy. Because of my pride and hot temper, I lost my daughter, and I've suffered eight years of torture, guilt and pain. And I've treated you badly, not only in the past, but since you returned to Greensboro." He paused, and his mouth twisted, as though the words were hard to speak. "I'm sorry."

"You were in the right, Mr. Weaver. I've never blamed you."

"No," Landon said, and he seemed to speak with an effort. "I was jealous of you, Nathan. Until you came along, Autumn was all mine. She had been from the day she was born. I couldn't bear to share her love with anyone. I wouldn't have minded if she married Dr. Lowe because I knew that I'd still be first with her, but when I fired you, and she told us that she intended to leave with you if you'd take her..."

"Did she tell you that?" Nathan interrupted, and the thought of what he'd missed brought a pain to his heart he'd never before experienced.

"That day I ordered you off our place, she came to Woodbeck Farm to go away with you, but you'd already gone."

"I didn't think she cared that much about me!"

"Neither did I, but her actions proved we were both wrong. When she ran away, I knew I'd made a big mistake. More than once, I wished I could beg her forgiveness, but when she returned I was still too proud to bring her home. Without Autumn, I didn't much care what happened to my farm, because she loved it as much as I did. I'm trying to make restitution for my past wrongs, Nathan. Keep the filly."

Nathan nodded agreement. "But will you go to Autumn, Mr. Weaver? Her love for you has never changed."

"I intend to make things right with her before this day is over. I'll confess to her that I'd told you she was going to wed Dr. Lowe. That wasn't exactly the truth. My wife thought it would be a good match, but Autumn was never interested."

Landon turned toward the truck, and as Jeff started the engine, he said over his shoulder, "I might add that Noel belongs to Autumn, and the mare will go wherever Autumn chooses to live. Good luck with your Belgian herd.''

Landon's words astonished Nathan so much he couldn't speak, and his legs felt weak. He leaned on his new filly and watched the truck and trailer leave the grounds.

''Cupid,'' he said, and the filly twitched her ears, ''did my ears deceive me, or was he giving me permission to marry his daughter?''

The filly nipped his shoulder and started toward the pasture. Still in shock, Nathan ambled along as Cupid made herself at home.

In late evening Autumn drove in and parked beside the porch, where Nathan sat surveying his farm. She wore a blue blouse, white skirt and sandals. Her brilliant hair was piled on top of her head, held in place with two ornate combs. Her blue eyes glistened, and her face wore the happy expression he hadn't seen for a long time.

He went down the walk to greet her and took her hand. ''If you stopped by for a meal, you're too late,'' he joked.

''Nope. I ate Miss Olive's food. She's a better cook than you are.''

''You never did tell me what kind of cook you are.''

''Probably a lousy one. I've never had a chance to find out.''

He pulled her close, and she sighed. ''Nathan, it's so good to be with you.''

This lighthearted exchange reminded him that they'd never had many carefree hours together. They hadn't had the advantage of a normal relationship. When he'd first known her, most of their meetings had been so fraught with tension, unrequited love, anger and disappointment that they didn't have many precious memories to cherish.

"Then if you're not hungry, I suppose you came by to see my new filly."

"As a matter of fact, I did. At least, that's one reason I came."

Keeping one arm around her waist, he steered her toward the pasture field where Cupid grazed.

"Daddy came today and apologized for the past, and I had a lot of apologizing to do, too. It's such a relief to forgive and be forgiven. He told me what he'd done."

"I didn't want to take the filly, but I realized I had to be a good receiver, that he had to make some tangible gift to show his change of attitude. Did he tell you she's Noel's foal?"

"Yes, which was a good choice, for you've helped save Noel's life twice."

Although Autumn exclaimed delightedly over the filly, try as she might, the animal would have nothing to do with her. She skittered out of the way when Autumn approached, but Nathan could walk up to her and she leaned contentedly against him. When Autumn finally gave up trying, he said, "She's definitely a one-man filly. Sorry."

Cupid would have followed Nathan out of the gate, but he pushed her gently aside and whispered in her ear, loud enough for Autumn to hear. "There's another female who has first dibs on my attention tonight."

Joining hands, they walked back to the house and sat together on the porch swing, where they faced the hazy sun which was slowly setting behind the trees along Indian Creek. Nathan put his arms around her, and for a long time their warm kisses and caresses chased away the bitterness of the past. They talked of the loneliness and frustration they'd endured because of their unrequited love, marveling that the affection between them that wouldn't die had slowly erected a bridge they'd finally crossed to happiness.

"Do you have any doubts now that the 'other' female in your arms is also a one-man filly?" Autumn murmured when her lips were free.

"I should have realized it before. I've been wondering today what our lives might have been if we'd gone away together. We'll never be able to make up for the years we've missed."

"I've wondered, too, if we would have found the happiness we wanted. I was immature, and I believe now that God knew best. I wouldn't want to repeat the miserable years I endured, but perhaps it was better for us. God has been orchestrating our lives all along."

Nathan caressed her hair, nuzzled her throat and nibbled on one ear.

"I came to a momentous decision the night my filly died. I thought my dreams of a Belgian herd was dead, but I didn't intend to let my other dream die. I love you, Autumn, and I have since the first time I saw you in the Weaver barn. Will you stay at Greensboro and marry me? I want to share your life. Will you stay with me? Will you?"

"Yes, Nathan. I love you, too. I don't think my parents will offer any objections now, but it doesn't matter. I believe the biblical teaching, 'A man will leave his father and mother and be united to his wife, and the two will become one flesh.' You'll come first with me from now on. I don't ever want to be separated from you again.''

Before the sun dipped below the horizon, it cast one last golden ray on the area where they sat, touching her hair and turning it into burnished bronze.

Nathan fondled the curly tresses he'd always admired, and whispered, "Let the past go. Tomorrow is a new beginning.''

Epilogue

The three Weaver daughters had been reunited, and the gazebo in the backyard was decorated for a wedding. Resplendent in a black tux, Landon Weaver sat on the driver's seat of the black barouche pulled by two Belgians and waited for the wedding procession to start. Tulip and Noel looked majestic in their black harness ornamented with silver, but Noel was the most festive. Autumn had braided pink carnations into the manes of both mares, but she'd tied a large pink ribbon around Noel's neck. After all, if it hadn't been for Noel, she and Nathan might never have met.

Fluffy white clouds decorated the blue October sky, and the sun shone brightly on the wedding party. Autumn, wearing her mother's wedding dress, sat on the rear seat of the barouche. When Landon turned to look with pride at his offspring, she blew a kiss in his direction, thankful that her father was once again the strong, vibrant man he'd been in her youth. Spring and Summer looked as radiant as Autumn, and it was little wonder Landon was proud of his daughters today.

Spring and her husband, now on missionary assignment in North Carolina, had come for the wedding, bringing their two children. Summer looked happier than Autumn could remember. She planned to leave the following week for a new job in New York City, where she would also continue her education.

The triumphal fanfare sounded, Landon lifted the reins, and the two Belgians moved forward in regal procession. For a moment, Autumn's mind flickered over the past few years. She'd traveled a long way physically, emotionally and spiritually since the day she'd met Nathan. It was difficult not to dwell upon what might have been, but the mutual love she and Nathan now shared was worth the wait. Perhaps their love was even deeper because they'd gone through so many years of frustration and denial.

The two months since the strangles epidemic had swept the community had brought many changes. Autumn had agreed to work with Ray at the clinic, expecting to become a full partner within a year. She'd moved back into her room at Indian Creek Farm, and Nathan had been a frequent visitor. Landon had offered Autumn and Nathan an interest in the farm, but Nathan had declined.

"Someday when you're not able to carry the full load, I might do that," Nathan said, "but I'd rather spend the next few years improving Woodbeck Farm. I'll appreciate your advice for that." With Noel and Cupid both in their possession, Autumn and Nathan intended to start their own herd of Belgians.

Clara waited for them at the gazebo. She sat in her wheelchair behind the assembled guests, but she'd declared that she would not be pushed down the aisle at her daughter's wedding. For the past two months, she'd been involved in a strict physical regimen until she could walk a short distance. David Brown, who'd come to Greensboro to see his brother Bert, had been pressed into last-minute service as an usher.

David stood beside Clara's chair, and when Landon brought the barouche to a halt, Clara painfully rose from the chair and clutched David's arm. When she might have fallen, he put his arm around her waist and carefully guided her to the front row of chairs. David sat beside Clara, and when the wedding party was in place, he lifted her and supported her as she watched Autumn glide down the aisle on Landon's arm. Autumn stopped to kiss Clara and whisper, "I love you, Mother."

With a happy heart and glowing face she moved forward to Nathan, who waited for her with Bert Brown standing beside him. When the time arrived for the father to give his youngest daughter away, Landon cleared his throat huskily a time or two before he could speak.

"I've never really wanted to give Autumn to anybody," he admitted, "but I want her to be happy, and so I give her to you, Nathan. She's wanted you long enough."

His comment brought a subdued titter from the audience, and Landon enveloped his youngest daughter in a fierce bear hug before he placed her hand in Nathan's. Autumn's eyes glowed with happiness as she and Nathan turned toward Pastor Elwood and took their vows.

* * * * *

Look out for Summer's story in
SUMMER'S PROMISE
Available from Love Inspired
in Fall 2001

Dear Reader,

The underlying theme of this book is forgiveness, and during the writing I gave a lot of thought to the subject. As my characters wrestled with their need to forgive and be forgiven, I considered the wonderful news of God's grace and how willing He is to forgive our sins. Perhaps the hardest words for anyone to say are "I was wrong," and/or "I'm sorry." However, before the cleansing power of forgiveness can transform our lives, we must be sincerely sorry for our sins, whether they've been committed against others or against God.

We often seek forgiveness from others by doing things for them—giving them something, as in the case of Landon when he gave Nathan a filly to replace the one he'd lost. The Bible teaches that it is sometimes necessary to make a tangible restitution to those we've wronged (*Luke* 19:1-10). Yet there's absolutely nothing we *can* do to receive God's mercy.

Consider a verse from the writings of the apostle Paul. "But because of his great love for us, God, who is rich in mercy, made us alive with Christ even when we were dead in transgressions—it is by grace you have been saved" (*Ephesians* 2:4-5). If you have not yet received the grace of God into your heart, I pray that this book will point you to Jesus, and His power to forgive.

My next Love Inspired book will continue the Weaver tradition through Summer Weaver, a sister to the heroine in this book. If you want to contact me, my address is: Irene B. Brand, P.O. Box 2770, Southside, WV 25187.

Irene B. Brand

Take 2 inspirational love stories FREE!

PLUS get a FREE surprise gift!

Special Limited-Time Offer

Mail to Steeple Hill Reader Service™

In U.S.	In Canada
3010 Walden Ave.	P.O. Box 609
P.O. Box 1867	Fort Erie, Ontario
Buffalo, NY 14240-1867	L2A 5X3

YES! Please send me 2 free Love Inspired® novels and my free surprise gift. Then send me 3 brand-new novels every month, which I will receive months before they appear in bookstores. Bill me at the low price of $3.74 each in the U.S. and $3.96 each in Canada, plus 25¢ delivery and applicable sales tax, if any*. That's the complete price and a saving of over 10% off the cover prices—quite a bargain! I understand that accepting the books and gift places me under no obligation ever to buy any books. I can always return a shipment and cancel at any time. Even if I never buy another book from Steeple Hill, the 2 free books and the surprise gift are mine to keep forever.

303 IEN CM6R
103 IEN CM6Q

Name	(PLEASE PRINT)	
Address	Apt. No.	
City	State/Prov.	Zip/Postal Code

* Terms and prices are subject to change without notice. Sales tax applicable in New York. Canadian residents will be charged applicable provincial taxes and GST. All orders subject to approval. Offer limited to one per household.

INTLI-299   ©1998